An Act of Love

Eileen Lanahan

NEPPERHAN PRESS, LLC
YONKERS, NY

Published by Nepperhan Press, LLC
P.O. Box 1448, Yonkers, NY 10702
nepperhan@optonline.net
nepperhan.com

PUBLISHER'S NOTE
This is a work of fiction. Names, characters, places, and incidents
are the product of the author's imagination or are used fictitiously,
and any resemblance to actual persons, living or dead, events, or
locales is entirely coincidental.

Printed in the United States of America

Library of Congress Control Number: 2010927715

ISBN 978-0-9794579-8-2

For my mother

Whoever is without love does not know
God, for God is love.

1 John 4:8

Henley-on-Hudson, 1987

ONE

KERRY AND HER friends were sitting in the stands, watching the basketball game. They were playing Dobbs Ferry for the championship, and with less than two minutes left in the game the score was tied.

"Come on," Amanda said impatiently.

"Get some points," Susan said.

"Take the ball away from them," Lisa said.

Kerry said nothing. She watched the boys struggling on the court. In particular, she watched Brian Donahue, the star of their team. Brian, who had wavy black hair and striking blue eyes, was the most attractive, most admired boy in the school. She liked watching him, but she had no illusions: she wasn't pretty, she wasn't smart, and she wasn't talented, so he would never be interested in her.

"Oh, look. He's got it," Amanda said.

Brian had just stolen the ball, and he quickly passed it to Mark, who was Susan's boyfriend. Mark had no one between him and the basket, but a Dobbs Ferry player overtook him and cut him off and stalled him in the corner.

Then seeing Brian in the clear, Mark passed it back to him, and Brian drove in for a layup. A Dobbs Ferry player went up to block it, and they collided.

Thrown off balance, Brian landed hard on the floor. And Kerry winced.

The referee blew his whistle, the game was stopped, and players from both teams gathered around Brian. The coach rushed out, followed by the manager.

"Oh, shit," Amanda said.

"That's just our luck," Susan said.

"They should call a foul," Lisa said.

Kerry said nothing. Praying for Brian silently, she watched as the ring of players opened and he appeared. He was on his feet. The coach was handling his right arm, carefully moving and turning it. And Brian was just staring at it.

When the coach led him off she could tell from his eyes that he was in pain.

A big man in a tweed jacket, who acted like a doctor, met Brian and examined his arm. The coach stood by. The man shook his head as if it was nothing.

Brian got a towel and wiped off his face, then jogged back out onto the court.

Everyone cheered, including people on the other side.

Kerry wondered if the doctor was right. From what she had seen in Brian's eyes, she believed his arm was seriously injured, maybe even broken. And she felt they shouldn't let him keep playing.

The referee called a foul, and Brian stepped to the free throw line. He took the ball from the referee and bounced it a few times. And then he aimed and shot the ball, which swished through the basket.

People cheered wildly, and they cheered again when Brian made his second free throw.

Dobbs Ferry came back and tied the score.

"Come on," Amanda said.

Brian took a pass and expertly dribbled around the boy who was covering him and made a jump shot, putting them into the lead again.

While people cheered, Kerry imagined how much it had hurt to make that shot.

Dobbs Ferry came back, but Brian blocked the shot and seized the ball and hurled it to Mark, who had broken away. This time Mark scored.

Again, while people cheered, Kerry imagined how much it had hurt to pass the ball like that.

With time running out, Dobbs Ferry came back again and made a shot that rebounded off the backboard. Their center jumped to tip it in, but Brian beat him, snatched the ball, and having no one open to pass to, dribbled it all the way up the court and made a layup, clinching the game.

"We did it!" Amanda said.

"We beat Dobbs Ferry!" Susan said.

"We won the championship!" Lisa said.

Kerry said nothing. She watched the people thronging out onto the court, surrounding Brian and patting his back. Before she lost sight of him, she caught a look of pain in his eyes that made her heart go out to him.

They met the boys in the parking lot: Kevin, who was Amanda's boyfriend, and Jerry, who was Lisa's, and Richard, who wasn't anyone's. Amanda had asked Kevin to bring him along in the hope that something might happen between him and Kerry, who had never had a boyfriend. But she didn't think Richard was interested in her. At least he didn't act like he was.

Kevin had his car, a bright red Cougar, and Jerry and Richard were taping streamers to it. Someone had made a sign, using cardboard and spray paint, which said: "WE'RE NUMBER ONE! THE HENLY HORNETS." And Kevin was holding it.

"Where should I put this?" he asked.

"On the windshield," Lisa said.

"That's a great idea, but how would I see?"

"You don't have to see. Amanda can tell you where you're going."

"Yeah. I guess. She does anyway."

They finally put the sign on the back.

A few minutes later Mark joined them with wet hair.

Susan greeted him and hugged him, saying: "You guys were fantastic."

"Brian was," Mark said.

"How's his arm?" Amanda asked.

"He says it's all right. But the coach wants him to get an X-ray, just to make sure."

"If his arm was broken," Lisa said, "the doctor would have noticed."

Mark looked blank. "What doctor?"

"The man who examined him."

"That wasn't a doctor. That was his father."

"I thought it was a doctor."

"I did too," Amanda said.

"Well, it was his father," Mark assured them. "He's always at the games."

Kerry said nothing. She had thought it was a doctor too. But she had seen the look in Brian's eyes, and now she believed even more that his arm was seriously injured.

"Come on. Let's go," Kevin said.

"Yeah. Let's give it to Dobbs Ferry," Richard said.

They all got into the car, with Amanda in front between Kevin and Mark, and the rest of them in back. Susan was in the middle, with Lisa sitting on Jerry's lap and Kerry on Richard's.

She wasn't used to having physical contact with boys. She still hadn't kissed one, while her friends were all beyond that point. She had always been behind her friends, starting with the fact that she had been born in December. She had always been younger and less mature.

"I hope I'm not too heavy," she said to Richard, whose legs had shifted under her.

"Oh, no. You're light."

"This one isn't," Jerry said.

"I only weigh a hundred," Lisa said.

"You weigh more than that," Kevin said.

"How would you know?"

"You're the same height as my sister, and she weighs a hundred and ten."

"Well, she has a bigger ass."

"She does?" Jerry said, sounding interested.

"If I catch you with his sister," Lisa said, "you won't get anything more from me."

Kerry always felt left out when they talked about sex. And

sitting on the lap of a boy she didn't know very well, she felt embarrassed.

They roared down Farragut and turned onto Broadway.

As they approached Dobbs Ferry they saw some people on their way home from the game, and Kevin honked the horn while the rest of them yelled out through the windows: "We're number one! We're number one!"

Kerry yelled along with them, but remembering the look of pain in Brian's eyes, she couldn't put her heart into it.

When she got home she found her brother Bobby in the kitchen. He was sitting at the table, having cookies and milk. He was two years younger, and his only interest in life was sports.

"Were you at the game?" he asked, still excited.

"Yeah," she said, sitting down with him. She reached for a cookie and took a bite.

"Did you see how Brian won it for us?"

"Yeah. I did."

"You know," Bobby said as if he was sharing top secret information with her, "he was playing with a broken arm."

She stopped chewing. "He was?"

"Oh, yeah."

"How do you know?"

"I was over at Scott's, and his brother told us. He took Brian to get an X-ray."

So she had been right.

"He won the game," Bobby said in awe, "with a broken arm."

"Yeah," she said. But she was thinking more about his pain than about his glory.

At that moment she heard their father on the back steps. She got up and opened the door for him, guessing that he had bags of groceries. Their father did all the food shopping and all the cooking. He didn't seem to mind doing it. In fact, he seemed to like it.

"Thanks," he said. "How are you doing?"

"I'm doing fine," she said, smiling. "Are there any more bags in the car?"

"No. I have them all."

"Guess what," Bobby said as their father set the bags on the table. "We beat Dobbs Ferry. We won the championship."

"We did? That's great," their father said. "It's the first time in many years."

"How many years?" Bobby asked as if it was a vital statistic.

"I don't know. It's the first time since we moved here."

"Can we shoot baskets?"

"Sure. You want to join us, Kerry?"

"No, thanks. I'll put the groceries away."

"You're a treasure," her father said, putting his arm around her shoulder and kissing her head.

Bobby got the ball from under the table and took a stance as if he was going to pass it or shoot it. His father made a quick move and stole it from him, then dribbled it across the kitchen and out the back door. Bobby ran after him, saying: "You traveled."

While she put the groceries away, Kerry thought about Brian, who would have his arm in a cast by now. She knew what that was like since she had broken her arm. She had done it skating. She was with Amanda and Susan and Lisa, who were all better skaters. She was trying to keep up with them, going around a turn, when she fell on the ice. It really hurt, but not wanting to spoil their fun, she pretended it was all right, and she kept skating. So she could understand why Brian had kept playing.

When she was done with the groceries she cleared the table and washed the glass that Bobby had used. She watched her father and her brother through the window. They were playing on the driveway. Bobby had the ball, and her father had him blocked in a corner. Bobby took aim and made a long shot through the hoop.

"Good shot," her father said proudly.

Kerry wished she was good at sports. She wished she had inherited her father's athletic ability. He had tried to teach her, but she just hadn't been able to learn how to shoot a basket or hit a baseball or catch a football. He had told her not to worry, that she would be good at other things. But so far she hadn't found anything she was good at.

She was lying on her bed, listening to a tape of Madonna.

Her mother appeared in her doorway. Her mother was wearing a gray suit and carrying her hefty briefcase. Her mother always brought work home.

"Hi," her mother said, out of breath from climbing the stairs. "Are you ready?"

"Yeah." On Friday they always went out for dinner.

"Then please tell your father and Bobby to stop. I don't want to wait for a table."

"Okay," she said, raising herself from her bed.

Her mother went to change.

Kerry went into the bathroom that she shared with her brother. She looked in the mirror and sighed, discouraged. She brushed her hair, trying to make it look halfway decent. Her hair was neither blond nor red but a color that Amanda said was strawberry blond. And right now it was dull and lifeless, as they said in the shampoo commercials.

Finally giving up, she went down to the kitchen and out the back door. She watched her father and Bobby for a moment, and then she called out to them: "Mom wants you to stop."

"Okay," her father said.

"Just one more shot," Bobby said. "I'll show you how Brian clinched the game."

"You'll have to get around me," his father said.

Bobby dribbled in, feinted to the left, and then darted to the right around his father and made a layup. Grinning, he said: "That's how he did it.'

"That was good."

"Except that he did it with a broken arm."

As they tromped into the kitchen, her father asked: "Where do you want to go for dinner?'

"Sam's," Bobby said. "I want pizza."

"What about you, Kerry?"

"That sounds fine."

"Well, let's see where your mother wants to go."

"She'll want to have Chinese," Bobby said. "And I don't want Chinese tonight."

"You wouldn't want crispy shrimp?"

"I don't know. Maybe."

"Or fish filet with ginger sauce?"

"I wouldn't mind. But I'd rather have pizza."

"What about you, Kerry?"

"I don't care."

While their father went to see how their mother was doing, Kerry and her brother went into the family room. Bobby turned on the television and switched channels, using the remote. He found a program that was giving the sports news.

"They should have covered our game," he said. "It would have made a great story."

Kerry said nothing.

They went to Sam's for pizza. Sam's was in Dobbs Ferry, and it had a bar, an informal dining room, and a formal dining room. It also had a separate door for takeout.

They sat in the informal room, at a corner table, and they ordered two small pies, one with mushrooms and the other with pepperoni. They didn't have a combination since Bobby didn't like mushrooms and their mother didn't like pepperoni.

"What would you like to drink?" the waitress asked. Like all the waitresses, she had black pants and a white blouse. Like all of them she had big hair, which was tied back in a pony tail.

"I'll have a Coke," Bobby said.

"What about you, Kerry?"

"A Coke," she said.

"That's two Cokes," her father summarized, "a Rolling Rock, and a half carafe of white wine."

"Okay," the waitress said, rushing off.

Kerry looked after her, admiring her hair. It had body and curl and vitality. It had, in such abundance, what her own hair obviously lacked.

While they waited for their drinks, her mother asked: "How was school today?"

They all could have responded to the question since Kerry and Bobby attended school, and their father taught high school in Yonkers.

"The kids were full of beans," their father said with affection.

"I wish I could say that about my clients," their mother said. She worked for a law firm in the city. In fact, she was a partner. And she was always involved in deals.

"What's happening with the big acquisition?"

"It might not happen. Our target found a white knight."

"What's a white knight?" Bobby asked.

"It's someone who rescues a company from being taken over by another company," their mother explained.

"By a company they don't like," their father added.

"Is someone who rescues you from losing a basketball game a white knight?"

"I guess he would be," their mother said.

"Then Brian is a white knight."

"Brian? Who's Brian?"

"The boy who scored the winning points against Dobbs Ferry," their father said.

"Oh. I see," their mother said.

"He did it," Bobby said, "with a broken arm."

"He must be crazy."

"He's a hero."

"He still must be crazy to play with a broken arm."

"He didn't know it was broken."

"It happened toward the end of the game," their father said, evidently having heard every detail from Bobby. "There were only a few minutes left."

"There were less than two minutes left. A boy from Dobbs Ferry knocked him down, but he got up and kept playing."

"He must have been in pain," their mother said.

"He was," Kerry said, breaking her silence.

They all looked at her in surprise.

"How do you know?" Bobby asked.

"I could tell from his eyes. And I know how it feels to break your arm."

"He shouldn't have kept playing," their mother said.

"But if he hadn't," Bobby said, "we wouldn't have won the championship."

"Well, winning isn't everything. Remember that."

Their father smiled at their mother as if he hoped she would apply that to her work, which she took very seriously.

They were at Amanda's house, in a room that would have been in the basement except that the house was built on a hillside, so the room had windows.

It was Saturday, and the four of them were hanging out, listening to music. Amanda was sitting on the floor, painting her toenails. Lisa was reclining on the long chair, leafing through a magazine. Susan was dancing, singing along with the music. And Kerry was gazing out the window, enjoying the view of the Palisades.

"What are we going to do tonight?" Amanda asked.

"We can go to my house," Lisa said. "My parents are going into the city."

"That sounds fine."

"I'll bring my new tapes," Susan said.

Kerry felt left out since she didn't have a boyfriend. Of course she was always welcome to join them, but after they had paired off, it wouldn't be much fun.

"Hey, Kerry," Amanda said. "Should I ask Kevin to bring Richard?"

She didn't think he was interested in her, but she was willing to try it. "Okay."

Amanda finished her little toenail, and then she called Kevin.

Kerry already wished she hadn't accepted the offer, and she hope Richard wasn't available.

But after hanging up, Amanda said: "Richard's coming."

"He must be interested in you," Lisa said.

"Yeah. He must be," Susan said.

Kerry wondered.

"You know," Amanda said, studying her. "You should wear your hair shorter."

"I should?"

"Yeah. It would look better."

"She's right," Susan said.

"I could cut it for you," Amanda offered.

"Oh, I don't know."

"Let her," Lisa said. "She'll do a good job. She always does mine."

Having nothing to lose, Kerry said: "Okay."

She sat in a chair with a sheet draped over her while Amanda carefully combed and snipped. And she wondered what she was going to look like.

"Now, isn't that better?" Amanda said, standing her in front of the powder room mirror.

"Yeah. It is," Kerry said, pleased.

"You look completely different," Susan said.

"Richard won't recognize you," Lisa said.

She was encouraged.

When she got home her father and her brother were out in the driveway, shooting baskets. Her father had the ball, but seeing her, he paused. "Who cut your hair?"

"Amanda did," she said, hoping he liked it.

"It really looks great. You're a pretty girl."

She glowed with the compliment.

"Come on," Bobby said impatiently.

"Okay," his father said, bouncing the ball and moving forward.

She went into the house and upstairs. She noticed that the door of her mother's office was closed. On Friday her mother brought home work from her office, which she did on Saturday and Sunday. Her father brought home papers to correct, but he did that late at night. Because he had an easier schedule, her father did the work of running the house, except for the cleaning. Her mother had a woman who cleaned the house, though for some reason she insisted on doing the laundry, which she did on Saturday. While the clothes were in the washer she worked in her office, and when the portable timer went off she went down and transferred the clothes to the drier. So doing the laundry hardly interrupted her legal work.

Kerry wandered into the bathroom and looked in the mirror. She really liked what Amanda had done, and she hoped it would make a difference with the boys.

She got ready for the evening. She took a shower and washed her hair. While it was drying, she examined her face. At least she had a good complexion, unlike some of the girls her age. She had only one incipient pimple, which she hid with makeup.

Then she put on her sexiest clothes and brushed her hair.

Downstairs, she found her father in the kitchen, preparing dinner. He had potatoes in the oven and steaks on a platter, ready for the broiler.

"Wow," he said, admiring her.

"Do I look okay?"

"You look terrific. Where are you going?"

"To a party at Lisa's."

"Then we better eat soon."

"Can I help you?"

"Yeah. You can wash the lettuce for the salad."

She was drying the lettuce when her mother appeared, saying: "I could smell the steaks. It was making me hungry."

Bobby joined them and asked: "Can we eat in the family room?"

"No," her mother said. "We're eating in the dining room, like civilized people."

"But there's a game on."

"You can tape it," her father said.

"Okay," Bobby said, leaving the kitchen.

Kerry turned and faced her mother, wanting her comment.

"Who cut your hair?" her mother asked.

"Amanda did," she said.

"I like it that way."

"You do?"

"Yes. It looks better."

"Come on," her father said. "We don't want to hold her up. She's going to a party."

"Where?" her mother asked.

"At Lisa's."

"Is someone picking up you?"

"No. I can walk there."

"I think your father should drive you."

"Why? It's not that far." She was afraid that if her father drove her, he would find out that Lisa's parents weren't there. And that would ruin everything.

"She can walk there," her father said. "As long as someone brings her home."

"Someone will," she assured them.

"Well, don't go on the aqueduct," her mother said.

"Don't worry. I won't." The aqueduct wasn't a safe place for girls to walk at night. They all knew that, and no one in her right mind would walk there at night.

When she arrived at Lisa's the boys were watching a basketball game, and the girls were sitting together, talking.

"What happened to your hair?" Jerry asked.

"Amanda cut it," Lisa said. "Doesn't it look nice?"

"Well, it looks different."

Richard glanced at her, and then he turned his attention back to the game.

Kerry joined the girls, who were talking about a movie.

"I still want to see it," Lisa said.

"Well, I don't," Amanda said.

"I don't either," Susan said.

"But don't you want to know what the war was like?"

"No," Amanda said. "I really don't."

Behind her, Kerry heard the boys talking.

"He broke the bone in his forearm," Mark said.

"Is that the tibia?" Kevin said.

"No, you idiot. The tibia's in your leg."

"Then what bone is it?"

"The radius."

"I thought it was the ulna," Richard said.

"It's one or the other," Jerry said. "They're both in your forearm."

"So how bad is it?" Kevin asked.

"The coach says it's pretty bad," Mark said. "It's broken in more than one place."

"Then he won't be able to play baseball."

"No. Not this season."

"Put on some music," Amanda said.

"Okay," Susan said. She got her cassette player and put on a tape of the Pointer Sisters.

"Turn that down," Mark said. "We can't hear the game."

Ignoring him, Susan started dancing. Amanda and Lisa followed her. Kerry hesitated, feeling self-conscious in front of Richard. But he wasn't paying attention to her, so she finally started dancing with her friends.

She liked to dance, but she had hardly ever danced with a boy. She almost wished the boys would continue watching the game since she was having a good time.

Eventually the boys joined them.

Richard danced with her, but he acted like he was only doing it because he was supposed to. And when Susan put on a slow number he wanted to sit down.

While the other couples danced, holding each other close, she tried to make conversation with him.

"What do you like to do?" she asked.

"Oh, I don't know. I like to go to movies."

"What have you seen?"

He mentioned a few, and without enthusiasm he started telling her the plot of one.

As she listened to him, she noticed that Susan and Mark were kissing. And now she really felt left out. She was here, with a boy, but he obviously wasn't interested in her.

Susan and Mark left the room.

"And then the good guy shot down the helicopter," Richard was saying.

A while later Amanda and Kevin also left the room. And finally Lisa and Jerry did.

"So that's how it ended," Richard said.

"Mm. Well—" She couldn't think of anything to say.

Richard evidently couldn't either, so they sat there for a while in silence. Then, as if he had suddenly noticed, he asked: "Where is everyone?"

"I don't know."

"Is the party over?"

Kerry shrugged. "I guess so."

"I'm kind of tired. If you don't mind, I'll take you home now."

"Okay," she said, having no choice.

As they left, he asked: "Should we tell anyone we're leaving?"

"No." She supposed that they were in different rooms around the house, and whatever they were doing, they didn't want to be disturbed.

"You're home early," her father said.

"I guess I am." She was standing in the doorway of the family room, where her father and her brother were sitting on the sofa, watching something on television. Richard had dropped her off as if he couldn't wait to get rid of her.

"Well, come and join us. We're watching Spencer."

"Okay," she said, needing reassurance.

Her father made a place for her next to him, and she settled into it. She leaned against him, laying her head on his shoulder, and he put his arm around her.

"Don't worry," he said. "You'll go to other parties."

"I'd rather stay at home with you."

"When you meet a boy you like, you'll want to be with him."

"I've met boys I like. That's not the problem. The problem is," she blurted out, "I haven't met a boy who likes me."

"Then there's something wrong with those boys," her father told her. "If they can't see how pretty you are, they're blind. Right, Bobby?"

"Yeah," her brother said dutifully.

Kerry appreciated her father telling her she was pretty, but she didn't believe it. If she were pretty, then Richard would be interested in her. Or some boy would be interested in her.

TWO

ON SUNDAY AS usual they went to the noon mass at Our Lady of the River. The church was in the center of the village, and Kerry's family could walk there in about five minutes. If they had taken the car to church, they would have had trouble parking since the noon mass was attended by a lot of people, including kids she knew from school.

In front of the church sheltered by a grotto was the statue of the Blessed Mother, holding the baby Jesus. In her face was a look of unconditional love, which Kerry would have liked to see in her own mother.

Going to church was one of the few things they did as a family, other than going out for dinner on Friday, and it gave Kerry a positive feeling, even though after they went home and ate pancakes her mother went back into her office for the rest of the day. At least for an hour they were all together.

They always sat in the same pew, in the same order. Her mother went in first, and then her brother, and then her, and finally her father, who genuflected deeply and crossed himself. She liked being next to her father, which enabled him to give her a complete hug as a sign of peace, whereas she could only reach past her brother and shake her mother's hand.

After communion her mother and her brother knelt for a brief prayer and then sat back, while her father remained on his knees, with his head bowed and his forehead against his clasped hands, until it was time to stand up for the final prayer. Kerry remained kneeling with her father since she had a lot of people to pray for, including herself. But today she devoted more than half of the time to praying for Brian. In particular, she prayed that his arm would fully recover so he could play sports again.

She had never seen Brian in church, though she assumed that he was Catholic since his last name was Irish. Maybe his mother wasn't Catholic, and that was why they didn't come to church as a family. Or maybe it was something else.

Concluding her prayers, she thanked God that her family went to church together.

On the way out they stopped and greeted Father Joseph, a kindly man with an Irish brogue who had always made her feel at ease. He had given her reassurance when she was preparing for her first communion and later for her confirmation. And unlike the temporary priests who passed through the parish, Father Joseph always remembered her.

Today he said: "Hi, Kerry. I like your new hair."

"Thanks, father," she said without blushing.

"It brings out the Irish in her," the priest said to her father.

"You mean the best in her," her father joked, shaking Father Joseph's hand.

She could tell that the priest would have liked to talk more with her father, especially about baseball, but there were people lined up behind them, so they moved on.

As they walked away from the church, her father said: "I liked his homily."

"It was all right," her mother said. "It was simple and clear."

"Well, I don't think a homily should be complicated."

"No, but it could be more sophisticated."

This conversation was typical of how her father and her mother differed. Of course it had started with their parents, her grandparents, who differed in the same way. Her father had been born and raised in the Bronx, where his parents still lived. His father had worked in construction, and his mother—after raising six children—had worked as a secretary at the phone company. With pride, her father called himself a BIC, which stood for Bronx Irish Catholic. He had gone to Catholic schools in the Bronx, and he had gone to Fordham for his bachelor's degree in English and his master's degree in education. And until about five years ago, he had taught at a Catholic high school in the Bronx.

In contrast, her mother had been born and raised in Connecticut. Her father owned a successful business, so her family had no money problems. She had gone to Wesleyan for her bachelor's degree in history and to Yale for her law degree. As a partner in the law firm, her mother made a lot more money than her father.

As she listened to her parents talk about the priest, she imagined asking them what was most important in their lives. Her father would have said: "My children and my students." Her mother would have said: "My work."

"Kerry," her mother said. "It's seven o'clock."

Reluctantly, she opened her eyes.

Her mother was standing over her, all dressed for work. She took the seven-nineteen train into the city. "You better get up."

"I will," she murmured. Of course it was the last thing she wanted to do.

"I have to go. I'll see you tonight." Her mother leaned over and kissed her goodbye.

Without moving she watched her mother stride out of the room. She couldn't imagine being like her mother, so competent and full of purpose.

After a while she raised herself and dragged herself into the bathroom. She sank onto the toilet and closed her eyes, completely relaxed. With her mother gone, she felt no pressure to get ready for school. She could have gone back to sleep right there, sitting on the toilet.

"Are you almost done?" her brother asked from the other side of the door.

"Yeah," she said. "Just a minute."

"Well, I don't want to be late for school."

"Okay, okay." She gave up the bathroom. She padded back into her room, wondering what to wear today. She finally put on her good jeans and her big blue sweater.

Down in the kitchen, she found her father, back from his run on the aqueduct. He was leaning against the counter with a glass of apple juice.

"Good morning," he said with emphasis on the first word.

"Good morning," she said. She couldn't imagine being like her father, so cheerful and full of energy.

"It's a beautiful day. It's clear and fresh, just perfect for running." He drank some juice. "And guess what. The crocuses are up."

"They are?" she said, heartened. The first sign of spring, her favorite time of year.

"I saw a few along the path."

"I'll look for them." She got the apple juice out of the refrigerator. "You want some more?"

"Yeah. Thanks."

She refilled his glass, and then she poured some for herself. She found a doughnut and sat down at the table.

Her father drank the juice, rinsed out his glass, and went to get dressed. He had to be at school by eight. And he always seemed eager to get there and be with his students. Whatever might have happened the day before, he started each day as if it was a new ballgame.

She wished she had his outlook. Today she would have liked to believe that things would be different, but she didn't see how they could be.

The last one to leave, she locked the back door and headed toward the gate. It led to the aqueduct, which went all the way from Croton to the city, making a path along the ridge that was ideal for walking. She used the path to go to school or to get away. Going north, she had followed it as far as Lyndhurst, and going south, as far as Greystone.

Walking along with her books in a backpack, she spotted some crocuses. They were purple, like the color the priest was wearing at mass now, with yellow stigmas. They made her happy. Just by appearing, by pushing up through the dead leaves, they gave her hope, and they confirmed her faith in God.

As soon as she had a full view of the river she stopped and gazed at it. In the morning sun the Palisades were all lit up, like a gold curtain, and the water was still. It gave her the feeling that the drama of her life was about to begin.

But nothing happened, so she continued walking.

She arrived at Five Corners, where the path was interrupted by streets. It continued on the other side of the intersection, passing the Episcopal church and skirting the ravine that divided the village. At this point she left the aqueduct and used the sidewalk, going uphill.

When she entered the school she was immediately oppressed by the familiar smell. And she was reminded of what she lacked since the school was where she had learned that she wasn't pretty, she wasn't smart, and she wasn't talented.

She went to the lockers and found her friends. They were hanging out, waiting for the bell.

"I really like your hair that way," Lisa told her.

"I do too," Susan said.

"I'm sorry about Richard," Amanda said.

"Oh, that's okay," Kerry said.

"I just found out that he likes Colleen."

At least that explained his lack of interest and made her feel a little better.

"Kevin should have told me."

"Boys are so dumb," Lisa said.

"They sure are," Susan said.

"Her parents won't let her go out with him," Amanda said.

"They won't? Why not?" Kerry asked.

"I don't know. I guess they don't like him."

"Well, I can see why," Lisa said.

"I can too," Susan said.

At that moment the bell rang, and lugging their books, they clomped to their homeroom.

There they separated since Ms. Bremen was fanatical about seating them in alphabetical order. Kerry sat in the fifth row between Pat McCain and Greg McKenna.

"Okay, okay," Ms. Bremen said, silencing them. Ms. Bremen had an authority that even the toughest boys respected. They said she had been an army drill sergeant, or that she was really a man in drag.

Ms. Bremen took attendance, rattling off their names. "Delucca? Where is he?"

No one seemed to know.

"Well, if he's goofing off—" Ms. Bremen warned. She left it for them to imagine what would happen. Then she continued: "Evans, Folino—"

Her mind wandering, Kerry remembered the crocuses, and she wished she was out on the aqueduct, away from here.

"McGrath? Sit up. I almost didn't see you. Are you trying to hide?"

"No," she stammered, sitting up.

A few people turned and stared at her, making her feel like a piece of shit.

Ms. Bremen finished, made some announcements, and then released them, except for Daniel Lieberman, who had arrived late. She wanted an explanation from him.

Kerry and her friends had geometry now, with Mr. Peters.

When they went into his room he was standing at the board, drawing some lines. They sat in the first row since at times he mumbled. Being right there in front of him, you were more likely to get called on, but in the back you couldn't understand him. And the subject itself was hard enough to understand.

Kerry had always gotten B's in math, though not without a struggle and help from Lisa. But geometry was something else. She just couldn't see it, and she couldn't understand why she had to learn it. All those lines and squares and triangles—she couldn't relate them to anything in the real world. And no one, including the teacher, could explain what it was all about.

Mr. Peters turned from the board and peered at them as if he was trying to identify them. He had a crew cut and thick glasses.

It took a while for the class to settle down, especially the boys in the last row.

"Okay," Mr. Peters said, swaying toward them. "Today we're going to prove the proposition that if two lines intersect, the angles formed by one of them are supplementary."

Kerry wrote down the proposition, but she didn't understand it. And even when Mr. Peters pointed out the angles on the board, she didn't see what he was trying to prove.

He did a few steps, and then he faced the class. "Can anyone tell me what to do next?"

She bent her head over her notebook.

"Kerry? Can you tell me?"

"No. I can't."

"Well, look at those lines." He turned to the board and pointed them out. "What do you see?"

"I see two lines."

Some people laughed.

"You don't see two angles?"

"Yeah. I see them. But I don't see anything special about them."

"Do you see how they're along this line?"

She nodded. "Yeah."

"And what kind of angle is a line?"

"I don't know. I don't see how a line can be an angle."

Some people laughed again.

"It's a straight angle, which has one hundred eighty degrees. Does that suggest anything?"

"No." She had no idea what he was getting at.

"Lisa," he said in exasperation. "Can you help her out?"

"Well, since the two angles are along the line," Lisa said, "their sum is equal to one hundred eighty degrees. Which makes them supplementary by definition."

"Right. Do you understand that, Kerry?"

"Yeah," she said, even though she didn't. She had already been embarrassed enough.

As they walked down the hall to their next class, Amanda said: "Don't feel bad. I didn't see it."

"I didn't either," Susan said.

"The only reason I did," Lisa said, "is because I read ahead in the book."

"I felt so dumb," Kerry admitted.

"You're not dumb," Amanda said. "You're just having trouble with geometry."

"And I am too," Susan said.

"Well, I don't want to flunk the course."

"You won't flunk it," Lisa said.

"Hey, look," Amanda said in a hushed voice. "There's Brian with his arm in a sling."

He was coming toward them with some other boys from the basketball team. He wore the sling, which formed a white triangle like a badge of courage.

"He broke it," Lisa said.

"He not only broke it," Susan said, "he broke it in more than one place."

"And he kept playing," Amanda said in awe.

They veered out of the way as the boys approached.

Kerry looked at Brian's arm, which was in a cast, and remembering what it had been like, she empathized with him. She looked up and met his blue eyes, staring at her. She felt like she had been caught snooping, and guiltily she looked away.

When the boys were out of hearing range Susan said: "I think he's the cutest boy in the world."

"Oh, I wouldn't go that far," Amanda said. "But he *is* cute. And he has a sexy mouth."

"He doesn't have a girlfriend," Lisa said.

"He hasn't ever had one," Susan said.

"I wonder why," Amanda said. "I mean, he could have any girl he wanted."

"Maybe he hasn't had time for girls," Lisa suggested.

"Playing three sports must keep him busy," Susan agreed.

"Mark only plays basketball, and during the season he doesn't have much time for me."

"Well, Brian will have time for girls now," Amanda said.

Kerry said nothing. She hadn't recovered from the way he had stared at her. She didn't know what it had meant. She only knew it had made her feel like somebody.

After lunch they had a study period, and Kerry was about to open a book when Ms. Bremen called her. She trudged up to the homeroom teacher's desk, conscious of people watching her and wondering what she had done.

"Ms. Davis wants to see you," Ms. Bremen said in a low voice, but not low enough. The people in the front row could have heard her.

"Now?" Kerry asked, stalling.

"Yes. Now."

With downcast eyes she left the room and headed for the guidance counselor's office. She hadn't ever gone there before, but she knew where it was.

When she opened the door Ms. Davis looked up from behind her desk. "Kerry?"

"Yeah." She stood in the doorway.

"Come in and sit down."

Warily, she advanced and sat down in front of the desk.

Ms. Davis had an anxious face, with short dark hair and intent dark eyes. She had creases in her forehead as if from worrying. "I got a note from Mr. Peters. He says you're not doing well in his class."

"I'm not," she admitted.

Ms. Davis looked down into a file. "You've always gotten B's in math. And you've gotten B's, and even some A's, in your other courses. So what's the problem?"

"I don't know. I just don't understand geometry."

"What don't you understand about it?"

"All those lines and squares and triangles— I can't relate them to anything."

"I know what you mean, but if you stick with it," Ms. Davis said encouragingly, "you'll see how it relates to algebra."

"I will?"

"You will. Have you told your parents you're having trouble with it?"

"I've told my father. And he tried to help me. But he had trouble with it too."

"What about your mother?"

"I haven't told her."

"Why not?"

"She's busy, and I don't want to bother her."

"What kind of work does she do?"

"She's a lawyer. She's a partner in a big firm in the city."

"Well, if you're having trouble with something, she's not too busy for you to tell her."

"I guess she's not."

"Then why haven't you told her?"

"I don't know. I guess I don't want to disappoint her."

"You're only having trouble with one subject."

"But I'm not good at anything."

"Yeah, you are. You get A's in English."

"They don't mean much."

"They mean a lot. You should be proud of getting those A's."

Kerry said nothing.

"You know," Ms. Davis said after a moment, "you're at an age when you're just beginning to find yourself. So open your mind about yourself. Be ready to discover things about yourself that you never imagined."

Kerry was skeptical, believing that the counselor said this to all the kids.

"Now, as for the geometry, Mr. Peters thinks you need a tutor."

"A tutor?"

"Yes. A person to help you."

"If I have a tutor, people will think I'm dumb."

"It doesn't matter what people think. If you don't have a

tutor, you'll keep having trouble, and you might end up failing the course."

"Okay," she said, accepting the tutor.

After school, while they were in the bathroom fixing their hair, Kerry told her friends why Ms. Davis had wanted to see her. And she told them how she felt.

"There's nothing wrong with having a tutor," Amanda assured her. "Jenny had one."

"An instructor from Fordham," Susan said.

"And he was cute."

Kerry felt better. With her friends supporting her, she didn't care what other people thought.

When they were ready they went to their lockers and got the books they were going to take home, and then they strolled out to the parking lot.

The boys were waiting for them. Kevin had his car, and Mark and Jerry were in the back seat.

As her friends got into the car, Kerry held back.

"Come on," Amanda said with the front door open. "You can sit with Kevin and me."

"I have to do some errands for my mother."

"You can do them later."

"No. I can't." Of course she wanted to go with them, but not without a boy. "I'll see you tomorrow."

"Okay," Amanda said, closing the door.

With a squeal of rubber the car roared off and left her behind in the parking lot.

She shouldered her backpack and headed home. She had no errands, she had nothing to do. She plodded down to the Five Corners and then got onto the aqueduct.

As soon as she had a view of the river she stopped and gazed at it. In the afternoon sun the Palisades were all in shadow, and the water was dark. It gave her a feeling of desperation, as if she was missing out on life.

Then something white caught her eyes. She looked and saw a

white triangle, a boy approaching, Brian Donahue.

Startled, she turned and continued walking.

"Hey, wait," he called.

She pretended she hadn't heard him since she couldn't believe he had spoken to her.

"Wait," he repeated.

Without stopping she glanced back over her shoulder. There was no one else he could have been speaking to, and he was walking quickly as if to catch up with her.

She finally stopped. She turned and waited, having no idea what he wanted.

"Are you in a hurry?" he asked, drawing near.

"No," she said, flustered.

"Then let me walk along with you."

She met his blue eyes, which made her feel like she really mattered, and she said: "Okay."

They started walking. The actual path, which had been worn by joggers, was only wide enough for one person. He let her have it, while he walked beside her on the grass.

"Where are you going?" he asked.

"Home," she said. She knew that in giving him only one-word answers, she must sound like an idiot. But she didn't think she could manage a complete sentence.

"Did you just move here?"

"No. I've lived here all my life."

"I don't remember seeing you before. I mean, before today in the hall."

"I have a new haircut. It makes me look different."

"It really must. I thought you were new."

Silently, she thanked Amanda.

"What's your name?"

"Kerry McGrath."

"I'm Brian Donahue," he said as if she wouldn't have known who he was.

"I know. I saw you win the basketball game."

"I didn't win it. The team did."

"And I saw you break your arm."

"Well, I didn't know it was broken."

"But it must have hurt."

"It did."

"I know. I broke my arm."

"You did? How?"

"I was skating. I fell on the ice."

"Did it heal all right?"

"I guess it did. It doesn't bother me."

"I hope mine heals all right."

"What does the doctor say?"

"He says it will."

"Then it will."

"I hope so." He sounded like he was worried about it. "How long was yours in a cast?"

"About six weeks."

"It's hard to do things with your arm in a cast."

"It is. I mean, like putting on a sweater."

"Or tying a shoe."

"Have you had an itch yet?"

"I had one today. It drove me crazy."

"You just can't think about it."

"No. You can't."

"But," she pointed out, "you have something to look forward to—having the cast taken off."

"I guess I do," he said with a smile.

They had reached her gate, so she stopped and said: "This is where I live."

They fell into a silence. All of a sudden they had run out of things to talk about.

"Well, I'll see you," he said finally.

"Okay," she said, wondering if he meant it. She opened her gate, but before she went into her backyard, she paused and gazed after him.

He was walking slowly, heading toward Dobbs Ferry as if he was in no hurry to get home.

He didn't look back.

The first to get home, she unlocked the back door and went into the kitchen. She put her backpack on the table, opened the refrigerator, got out the milk, poured a glass, and took a drink. She found the cookies, and nibbling one, she ambled to the front door and got the mail. As usual there was nothing for her, only bills and catalogs and junk, which she brought back to the kitchen and set on the counter.

She sat at the table and ate another cookie, thinking about her encounter with Brian. She was sure it had been accidental since he couldn't have known she would be on the path. She might have gone in the car with her friends. But when he saw her he called to her, he asked her to wait. So for some reason he wanted to meet her.

Of course that didn't mean he was interested in her. He had probably just been curious since he didn't remember seeing her before. He had probably just wanted to know who she was, and now that he knew, he was satisfied.

Still, it had been nice while it lasted, walking and talking with Brian Donahue.

The door opened and Bobby came in noisily.

"You're home early," he said.

"Yeah. I have a lot of work to do."

"Well, I hope you haven't eaten all the cookies."

"I haven't. I left one for you."

"One? Just one?" He grabbed the box.

She had been joking, but since she wasn't in the habit of joking, he had taken her seriously.

"Aw, you faked me." He took out a cookie and stuffed the whole thing into his mouth. He got a glass, poured some milk, and sat down with her. "You know, I saw Brian in the hall today. His arm was in cast."

"I know. I saw it."

"I wish I could sign it," Bobby said as if this would be the greatest honor.

"Why don't you ask him?"

"Oh, I wouldn't dare. I wouldn't dare talk with him."

She could have said she had talked with him, but if she had then Bobby would have told everyone. And she had decided to keep it a secret, even from her friends, since people might think she was having delusions.

On week nights she helped her father make dinner since her mother rarely got home before eight. If her mother caught the seven-twenty train, they would all eat together. But if her mother got home later, they ate without her.

Her father was a good cook, with a repertoire of cuisines ranging from Italian to Mexican, but her mother liked simple food and her brother was a picky eater who would have been happy eating pasta every night—noodles with butter since he didn't like sauces. When they had pasta her father made a sauce for the rest of them and kept Bobby's noodles separate, so all he had to do for Bobby was put a chunk of butter on them.

Tonight they were having penne a la Bolognese, which her father had taught her how to make. He would be home soon, but instead of waiting for him she began the sauce, starting with the onions. A big advantage of onions was that peeling and slicing them drove Bobby from the kitchen since he claimed they hurt his eyes.

She was browning a mixture of ground beef, ground pork, and ground veal in a cast-iron pan when the phone rang. It was her mother, who told her she wasn't going to make the seven-twenty train, so they should go ahead and eat without her.

Disappointed, Kerry went back to the stove and stirred the meat. At that point her father came in the back door, saying: "That smells good."

"Mom just called," she told her father. "She's going to be late."

"She's working on an important deal," her father said in justification.

"She's always working on an important deal."

"She loves her work."

"What about us?"

"She loves us. But she needs to work in order to fulfill herself.

If your mother didn't work, she wouldn't be happy. And that would affect us."

"I don't see how it would affect us. She's never here."

"Hey," her father said gently. "Did something happen at school today?"

"Yeah," Kerry said with her eyes on the pan. "I had a meeting with the guidance counselor, and she told me I need a tutor in geometry."

"Don't feel bad. I needed one too."

"You did?"

"Yeah. But I didn't have one. If I had, I would have learned more, and I could have helped you more."

"Why didn't you have one?"

"I didn't want people to think I was dumb."

"Well, I wish I didn't need a tutor."

"Don't worry about geometry. You're good at other things."

"What am I good at?"

"You're good at being a human being. And that's the most important thing."

Stirring the sauce, Kerry wondered if maybe that was what Brian saw in her. It was possible, but not likely.

She was in her room, studying geometry. She heard her mother climbing the stairs. It was after nine, so she must have taken the eight-twenty.

"Hi," her mother said, stopping in the doorway.

"Hi," she said, turning in her chair.

Her mother looked tired, but not unhappy. "I heard I missed a good dinner."

"It was just pasta."

"Well, I wish I could have joined you, but I had to stay late and work on that deal."

"That's okay."

"I also heard you're having trouble with geometry."

"Yeah," she admitted.

"Why didn't you tell me?"

"I don't know. I didn't want to bother you."

"It wouldn't have bothered me. Whatever it is," her mother said as if this was something very important, "whatever kind of trouble you're having, I want to know about it. So don't worry about bothering me."

"Okay," she murmured.

"Now, what about the tutor? Are they going to get one?"

"Yeah. They are. But we have to pay him."

"We can afford it."

"I'm sorry," she said, feeling that she was a burden to her mother.

"There's nothing to be sorry about. It's not your fault."

"I feel it is. I'm not good at anything."

"You're only beginning to find yourself. Remember, you're younger than the other kids in your class. You're still behind them, physically and emotionally."

"Then maybe I should drop back a year."

"Do you want to?"

"No. But maybe I should."

"I think you should keep trying to catch up. I know you will. And then you'll be glad you didn't drop back."

"Okay," she said doubtfully.

Later, while she was lying in bed, she thought about what had happened that day. She had messed up in geometry class. She had seen Ms. Davis. She had met Brian on the aqueduct. She had walked with him, she had talked with him. But she probably wouldn't meet him again. And she would have to see the tutor regularly.

THREE

THE NEXT DAY was St. Patrick's Day, so she put on her green sweater for the occasion, though she didn't need the sweater to proclaim her heritage—when people met her they could tell just by looking at her that she was Irish.

Arriving at school, she went to the lockers and found her friends. They were talking about what had happened yesterday after school.

"What if that guy had hit Kevin?" Lisa was saying.

"He would have been sorry," Amanda said. "Kevin's tough. Have you ever felt his muscles?"

"No. I haven't. But I guess you have."

Amanda smiled knowingly. "Yeah. I have. And if I were a boy, I wouldn't mess with him."

"I wouldn't either," Susan said. "And Mark could have handled that tall guy."

"Well, I don't know about Jerry," Lisa said.

"You don't think he could have handled the other guy?"

"I don't know, and I don't care. I think it would have been stupid for them to fight."

"I think it would have been exciting," Amanda said.

"What happened?" Kerry asked.

"Oh, we went to Carvel," Amanda explained. "We were in the car, eating our cones, when some guys pulled up alongside us. They made remarks about Kevin's car."

"They also made remarks about you," Susan pointed out.

"Yeah, one of them asked what a cool girl like her was doing with such a loser," Lisa said.

"So Kevin got out," Amanda went on, "and dared the guy to

repeat what he'd said. The guy got out—"

"They all got out," Susan said.

"—and he faced Kevin. He didn't repeat what he'd said, but he said he could prove it. So Kevin told him to go ahead."

"They stood there, glaring at each other," Lisa said.

"The guy finally said he could, but he wouldn't since he didn't want to hurt Kevin."

"And Amanda laughed."

"I couldn't help it."

"But that egged the guy on."

"I know it did. I wanted them to fight."

"I did too," Susan admitted.

"You're awful," Lisa said, disgusted with them.

"It would have been exciting."

"It would have been stupid."

"Well, they didn't fight," Amanda said. "The guy backed off and said he was going to buy some ice cream."

"Kevin called after him," Susan said, "that he should buy lemon because it was yellow."

"The guy ignored him," Amanda said.

"You see what you missed?" Susan said. "You should have come with us."

"I couldn't," Kerry said, glad that she hadn't. If she had, she would have missed Brian on the aqueduct. She was tempted to tell them about it, but she stuck by her decision to keep it a secret, as least for now.

Mr. Peters didn't call on her in geometry class. He acted as if he had done what he could for her, and now she was someone else's responsibility. She tried to follow him, but as usual she got lost. And she wondered if any tutor could help her.

They had French class next. They all took French instead of Spanish since Lisa had said it was more important. There was more literature, more philosophy, and more science written in French. Of course at this point they were a long way from being able to read it.

When you walked into Ms. Caldwell's room you had no doubt about what she taught. The walls were covered with posters that showed the Eiffel Tower, Notre Dame, the cathedral at Chartres, a street scene on the Left Bank, and a chateau on the Loire. Ms. Caldwell had lived in Paris for a while, and if you wanted to make her digress, you only had to ask her about it.

Kerry wasn't bad at French. At least she could read it and understand it. But she had trouble speaking it and writing it. And the worst thing about the class was when Ms. Caldwell made you go to the board and do a *dictée*.

Ms. Caldwell always began the class speaking French, telling them what day it was, what the weather was like, and what was happening in the world. She was an attractive woman, with natural blond hair. She wore stylish clothes, a different outfit every day. She didn't wear a wedding ring, which prompted speculation about her love life.

Today she began the class as usual, then asked questions, which they were supposed to answer in French. She directed a question at Lisa, who responded immediately in an accent that sounded perfect.

"Bon," Ms. Caldwell said, pleased. Then she called on Jim Reilly, who mumbled something unintelligible. "In French we have to enunciate. We can't be lazy, as we are in English. Now, try it again, Jim."

Jim mumbled something almost intelligible.

They had a lesson in adjectives, they learned some new vocabulary, they read aloud a passage from the book, and then Ms. Caldwell said: *"Bon, bon.* Now, let's do a *dictée."*

Kerry tried to become invisible.

But Ms. Caldwell spotted her and said: "Kerry, you haven't done one for a while."

She got up and walked slowly to the board, wishing they had delayed the *dictée* by asking Ms. Caldwell about Paris. She found a piece of chalk and faced the board. She could feel all their eyes on her, and she hoped she wouldn't make a fool of herself.

"Bon," Ms. Caldwell said. *"Je suis étudiante—"*

Kerry wrote the first three words, trying to decide whether to use an *accent grave* or an *accent aigu*. She finally guessed and waited for more.

"Is that how you want to write it?' Ms. Caldwell asked, hinting that there was an error.

Kerry looked at the words. The only possible problem she could see was the accent, which she started to erase.

"No, the accent's right," Ms. Caldwell said.

Kerry restored the accent, looked at the words again, and said: "I don't see a problem."

"Does anyone see a problem?"

"I do," Dan said smugly. "There should be an *e* at the end of *étudiante.*"

"There should? Why?" Ms. Caldwell asked.

"Because she's a girl."

"How do you know?" Steve asked.

"He saw her naked," Gary said.

The boys all laughed, and a few girls giggled.

Kerry was mortified. She hated Dan and Steve and Gary and everyone who had laughed or giggled. Above all, she hated Ms. Caldwell for making her do a *dictée.*

"Silence," Ms. Caldwell said in French. But she had lost control of them.

"He could have been wrong," Steve said.

"I guess he could have," Gary said.

"Grow up," Amanda said scornfully.

"We're not in kindergarten," Susan said.

"We're not," Lisa said. "But they should be."

The boys said nothing further.

"Bon," Ms. Caldwell said relentlessly. "Now, correct the gender of *étudiante.*"

Kerry did, and grateful to her friends for supporting her, she waited for the next phrase.

At recess they were standing in the hall, discussing what had happened in French class.

"Steve is an asshole," Amanda said.

"A super asshole," Susan said.

"None of the girls like him," Lisa said.

Kerry said nothing. She had only made a spelling mistake, but it had raised the issue of her sex, and if she was still so undeveloped that boys couldn't tell if she was a girl, then no wonder they weren't interested in her.

"Where should we go after school today?" Lisa asked.

"Let's go to Carvel again," Amanda said.

"I can't. I'm on a diet," Susan said.

"Since when?"

"Since yesterday."

At that moment she saw Brian coming down the hall. Afraid of making a fool of herself, she pretended not to see him. If he stopped and addressed her, she would happily respond to him. But she wasn't going to stand there in expectation and then have him walk right by her.

"I'm not seeing Kevin today," Amanda said. "He has to take his dog to the vet."

"Then let's do something without the boys," Susan said.

"Yeah, let's go shopping," Lisa said.

With her heart pounding, Kerry stared at the floor. She heard his footsteps, she caught a flash of white out of the corner of her eye. And she felt him go by her.

"No one has signed his cast," Susan said as soon as he was out of hearing range.

"How could you tell?" Amanda asked.

"Well, no one has signed on the part I could see."

"There might be something under the sling."

"You mean a secret signature?"

"Yeah. You never know."

Kerry gazed after him dejectedly. She had met him on the aqueduct, she had walked with him and talked with him, but that was it. There was nothing more.

After school they went into the village, crossing at Five Corners and heading down Main Street.

When they passed Sal's and smelled the pizza they decided to stop. They ordered two slices and a large Coke, which the four of them shared. They chatted with two boys who came in while they were hanging out there. One of the boys had graduated from their school last year and was now working as a plumber's assistant. He said he liked it.

Then they continued, stopping at the corner of Main and Warburton and looking in the window of the shoe store.

"I like those green ones," Amanda said, tapping the window.

"They're pretty," Susan said.

"But I don't have any clothes to wear them with."

"So why are you looking at shoes?" Lisa asked. "You don't have any clothes."

"Well, it's fun to imagine having clothes."

They turned on Warburton. They sauntered along, passing the stationary store, the new drugstore, and the diner, which always had people in it. They went into the only store in the village that had clothes for people their age, and they looked at things.

Kerry was drawn to a cotton sweater. She loved the color, rose pink. She checked and found that it was a small. She held it up in front of her.

"You'd look good in that," Amanda said.

"You think so?"

"Yeah. Try it on."

"Well, I probably can't afford it." She found the price, which had been marked down.

"How much is it?" Lisa asked.

"Nineteen ninety-five."

"Is it pure cotton?"

Kerry checked the label. "Yeah. It is."

"Then it's a good value."

"Try it on," Amanda urged her.

She went into the room behind a curtain where you tried on things and pulled off her top. For a moment she looked at herself in the mirror, relieved that she finally filled her bra. And then she tried on the sweater.

It fit her perfectly. It was comfortable but tight enough to show her breasts. And because of what had happened in French class, she wanted to show them. She wanted people to have no doubt that she was a girl.

She went out and displayed the sweater to her friends.

"You really look good in that," Amanda said.

"It's sexy," Susan said.

"For nineteen ninety-five," Lisa said, "you can't go wrong."

So she bought the sweater. That is, she gave the woman five dollars and asked her to hold it. She had to get the rest of the money from her father.

As she was leaving school the next afternoon she saw Brian standing on the sidewalk, adjusting his sling. He was so preoccupied that she could have slipped by him without being noticed, and she almost did. But at the last moment she decided to risk being slighted by him.

"Hi," she said without undue familiarity.

"Oh, hi," he said as if he was surprised to see her.

She didn't stop since he hadn't given her any reason to, but she did slow down. If he wanted to say anything more to her, he had a chance.

"Are you going home?" he asked.

"Yeah. But I have to do an errand first." By now she had stopped.

"Where? In the village?"

She nodded. "Yeah."

He gazed at her with those sheer blue eyes. "I have to do an errand myself. Do you mind if I walk with you?"

"No. I don't mind," she said as casually as possible.

They started walking toward the village.

"What do you usually do after school?" he asked.

"I usually hang out with my friends."

"Where?"

"Oh, anywhere. We go to someone's house, or we go for a ride in someone's car."

"Do your friends drive?"

"Amanda does. And so does Lisa."

"What about you?"

"I'm only fifteen." She wondered if she should have told him she was sixteen. She had a fake driver's permit to prove she was sixteen, which she had used on other occasions. But she decided that on this occasion she had been right to admit the truth about her age, whatever the consequences.

"Well, I can't drive now."

"I guess you can't."

"I wish I could. I wish I could get away from here."

"Where would you go?"

"Across the river."

"I haven't ever gone there."

"You haven't?"

"No. I've gone to the city, and I've gone to Connecticut, but I haven't ever gone across the river."

"When I can drive again, I'll take you there."

"Okay," she said, doubting he would.

"What did you do yesterday after school?"

"We went shopping. That's my errand. I bought a sweater, and I'm going to pick it up."

"I'm going to the drugstore."

She supposed it had to do with his arm.

But then he said: "I have to pick up drugs for my mother."

"Is she sick?"

"Yeah."

"What's wrong with her?"

"God knows," he said despondently.

Kerry didn't know what to say. She gathered that his mother didn't have cancer or anything like that, but whatever she had, it burdened him.

They reached Five Corners, and after waiting in silence for the light they crossed Broadway.

"Tell me about your friends," he said, changing the subject.

"Well, there's Amanda, who's very pretty. There's Lisa, who's very smart. And there's Susan, who's very talented."

"Is Susan the girl who goes with Mark?"

"Yeah. They've been going together for a long time."

"He talks about her. He says she has a beautiful voice."

"She does. She sings in the choir of my church."

"You mean Our Lady of the River?"

"Yeah. That's my church."

"It should be mine, but we don't go to church."

"Why don't you?" she asked after a moment of hesitation.

"My mother won't go anywhere."

"You mean she never leaves your house?"

"No. Unless it's an emergency," he added glumly.

She didn't ask what kind of emergency.

"Do Amanda and Susan have boyfriends?" he asked, again changing the subject.

"Yeah. Amanda goes with Kevin, and Lisa goes with Jerry."

"What about you?"

She realized now where he had been heading. "I don't have a boyfriend, if that's what you mean."

He was silent for a while, and then he asked: "Did you see me coming toward you in the hall yesterday?"

"Yeah," she admitted.

"Then why did you pretend you didn't?"

"I don't know. I guess I thought you'd walk right by me."

"Well, I thought you didn't want to talk with me."

She was amazed. The most attractive, most admired boy in the school had thought she didn't want to talk with him.

"You know," he admitted. "I wasn't standing in front of the school accidentally. I was waiting for you, I was hoping you'd come out."

She finally believed he was interested in her, but she couldn't imagine why. She decided he had illusions about her, and she wondered if she should tell him now what she was really like and get it over with.

"I shouldn't have walked by you yesterday," he said.

"I shouldn't have pretended I didn't see you," she said.

With this resolved, they walked together more comfortably.

When they arrived at the drugstore he said: "Come in with me. It'll only take a minute."

She followed him in, but respecting his privacy she stopped at the card rack while he went to the prescription counter. She heard the druggist greet him as if he was a regular customer.

"Are they ready?" Brian asked.

"Oh, yes. I have them. I was a little short on one of them, but I'll have more tomorrow if you want to drop by. Or I could have it delivered to you."

"I'll pick it up."

Brian didn't pay for the drugs, so his mother evidently had an account there. He took the bag from the druggist and slogged out as if he had forgotten about her.

Outside, he headed back toward Main.

"I have to pick up my sweater," she reminded him.

He pivoted around. "Oh, yeah. I'm sorry. I just get so upset by these drugs."

"What are they for?"

"They're for her mental illnesses."

"She has more than one mental illness?"

"Oh, yeah. She has them all. She has all the mental illnesses that were ever invented."

"Do the drugs help her?"

"They don't seem to. I mean, if you ask her how she is, she's never better."

"Maybe without them she'd be worse."

"Yeah. Maybe."

They continued walking until they arrived at the store where she had bought the sweater.

He followed her in and waited while she paid the balance with the money her father had given her. Then she held the sweater up for Brian to see.

"I like it," he said, brightening.

"I'll wear it tomorrow."

As they walked back up the hill toward the aqueduct he said: "My father wants me to go to baseball practice."

"He does? Why?"

"He says I can help the pitchers. But I don't see how. I can't show them how to throw a ball."

"Maybe you can tell them how to do it."

"But I don't think about how I do it. I just do it."

Of course she realized that if he went to baseball practice he couldn't meet her after school. But she didn't want him not to go on her account, so she said: "Well, maybe you should do what your father wants."

"I'm tired of doing what my father wants."

When they reached her gate they stopped and lingered.

"Can you meet me tomorrow after school?" he asked after a long silence.

"You're not going to baseball practice?"

"No. I'm going to do what *I* want."

"Then I can meet you. Where?"

"Where we met today."

"Okay," she said, daring to smile.

"I'll see you tomorrow," he said, looking happy.

Again, before going through her gate she paused and gazed after him.

And he looked back.

The next day at recess Kerry and her friends were standing in the hall, talking.

"I have my mother's car today," Amanda said. "We could go to White Plains."

"We could go to the Galleria," Susan said.

"I'd rather go to Bloomingdale's," Lisa said.

"We could go to both," Amanda said.

"I can't go," Kerry said.

"Oh, don't tell us you have to do an errand. It'll just be us. No boys."

"I still can't."

"Why can't you?" Susan asked.

She had to tell them something, but she wasn't quite ready to tell them everything. She was still afraid it wasn't what she hoped. "I have to meet someone."

"Who?" Amanda asked.

"Oh, someone," she murmured, trying to leave it at that.

"You have to tell us," Lisa said. "We don't have secrets from each other."

Ready or not, she had to tell them. They supported her, they encouraged her, they included her in things they did. And Brian might never have noticed her if Amanda hadn't given her a haircut. "I'm meeting Brian."

"Brian Donahue?" Amanda said.

"Really?" Susan said.

"What have you been up to?" Lisa asked.

They were surprised, but they believed it. They didn't act like it was unthinkable for Brian to be interested in her. And this gave her a real lift.

"Tell us about it," Amanda said.

"Well, there's not much to tell. As I was going home on Monday, I met him on the aqueduct. I mean, he saw me and called to me—"

They listened without interrupting her.

As she went on it occurred to her that she had never talked so much. She had never had anything to talk about.

Then, as if to confirm her story, Brian appeared. With Mark and another boy, he was coming toward them. And instead of walking by her, he stopped.

"Hi," he said to her.

"Hi," she said, elated.

School was over, and she was about to leave her homeroom when Ms. Bremen called her.

She marched up to the teacher's desk.

"Ms. Davis wants to see you."

"Now?"

"Yes. Now."

She walked quickly to the guidance counselor's office. She assumed that Brian was waiting for her in front of the school, and she hoped this wouldn't take long.

When she got there she saw Mr. Webb, the assistant principal, talking with Ms. Davis. She had to stand there for a long time while he went on and on about something in his nasal voice.

Ms. Davis finally cut him off, saying: "I have a student waiting to see me."

"Oh, all right," Mr. Webb said, glancing around.

"I'll talk with you later."

With a fatuous smile Mr. Webb ambled past her on his way out, smelling of mint.

"Come in," Ms. Davis told her.

Kerry went into the office but remained standing, trying to convey the fact that she didn't have much time.

"I'm sorry to keep you waiting," Ms. Davis said.

"Oh, that's okay," Kerry said.

"I've found a tutor for you. He's a retired math teacher from Irvington."

She was disappointed, having hoped for a young instructor from Fordham, though now that she had something going with Brian, she didn't care. She shrugged. "Okay."

"He can do it after school. Is that all right?'

She realized that if she did it then, she wouldn't be able to see Brian. "I'd rather do it on weekends. Could he do it then?"

"I'll call him and see," Ms. Davis said, reaching for the phone.

"Oh, I don't have to know right now."

"Why wait?" Ms. Davis said, dialing. "The sooner you get started, the better."

Anxious to go, she hoped the man wouldn't answer.

But he did answer, and after questioning him Ms. Davis determined that he couldn't do it on weekends, and anyway, he didn't think it would be as effective that way.

"What should I tell him?" Ms. Davis asked, holding her hand over the mouthpiece.

"I don't know. I have to think about it.'

After telling the man she would get back to him Ms. Davis hung up. "Well, you have to make a decision on this."

"I'll let you know tomorrow."

"All right." Ms. Davis finally let her go.

She bolted to her locker, grabbed her books, and raced down the hall. She rushed out the door and looked for Brian, ready to explain why she had kept him waiting.

But he wasn't there.

She checked her watch and figured that she had been delayed about twenty minutes. And that wasn't too long to wait for someone.

Assuming he had also been delayed, she waited for him. She stood where he had been adjusting his sling the day before. She paced a little, she checked her watch, and every time the door opened she hoped it was Brian, she prayed it was Brian. But it never was.

She waited an hour and then gave up. She trudged home, trying to understand what had happened. He had definitely asked her if she could meet him today after school, and she had said yes. She hadn't imagined it. They had a date.

Had he forgotten? Had he changed his mind? Had he already lost his illusions about her?

Whatever the reason, he didn't want to see her. And she didn't blame him. She blamed herself for thinking that Brian Donahue could ever have been interested in her.

FOUR

WHEN SHE ARRIVED at school the next morning she found her friends standing by their lockers. She greeted them and went to her locker, unable to hide her feelings.

"What's wrong?" Amanda asked.

"Oh, nothing," Kerry said, working the combination of her lock. She lost her place.

"Did you meet Brian yesterday?"

"No." She started over with her lock.

"Why not?" Susan asked.

"He didn't show up."

"That's strange," Lisa said.

"There must have been a misunderstanding," Amanda said.

She turned from her locker and faced them. "No. I'm sure he asked if I could meet him after school. And I said I could. So there wasn't any misunderstanding."

"Then something must have happened."

"He would have told me."

"Maybe he couldn't. Maybe he had an emergency."

She remembered his using this word yesterday. "Maybe. But I don't think so. I think he just didn't want to see me."

"Then why did he ask if you could meet him?" Amanda asked.

"I don't know. I guess he thought he wanted to see me, but he changed his mind."

"No, he didn't. Boys aren't like that. They know what they want."

"They sure do," Susan agreed.

"Well, then he forgot," Kerry said.

"No, he didn't," Amanda said. "He's probably looking for you right now, wanting to explain. So get your books, and let's go where he can find you."

She turned back to her locker and spun the dial. She still thought he hadn't wanted to see her, but she was open to the possibility that her friends were right.

They walked to the main hall and posted themselves opposite the front door.

A few minutes later Brian came in. He was heading toward them, but when he saw Kerry he swerved away and walked past them. There was no doubt that he was avoiding her.

"That's strange," Lisa said.

"I told you," Kerry said. "He doesn't want to see me."

"He apparently doesn't," Amanda said, puzzled. "But he did before. So what happened?"

"I don't know. I guess he found out how dumb I am."

"You're not dumb."

"I am compared with him."

"You're not. He may be smarter than you in some ways, but not in others."

"That's true," Susan said. "I mean, it's true about boys in general. They act like they know everything, but they really don't."

"They don't know a lot of things," Lisa agreed.

"I wonder what happened," Amanda said.

"I could get Mark to ask him," Susan offered.

"That's an idea. Do you want him to?"

"Well—" At least she would know, instead of guessing. "Yeah. Okay."

At that moment the bell jangled.

She was leaving the cafeteria with her friends, still not knowing what had happened.

Brian was standing in the hall. He was slouched against the wall, with his head drooping, and when he saw Kerry he came to attention and moved to intercept her.

"Can I talk with you?" he asked awkwardly.

"Yeah. Sure." She could guess what he was going to tell her, and she would have rather heard it through Susan.

"We'll see you later," Amanda said, patting her shoulder.

Her friends left her alone with him.

"Come on," he said as other people emerged from the cafeteria. "Let's go outside."

She followed him out the nearest exit. It led to a side street where recently some boys had been caught dealing crack. So people were avoiding the spot, not wanting to be thought guilty by association with it.

Brian faced her with contrite eyes and said: "I'm sorry. I should have waited longer for you."

"You waited for me?"

"I waited twenty minutes. And then I figured you'd gone off with your friends."

"You thought I wasn't going to meet you?"

"Yeah. That's what I thought. So I left and went to baseball practice."

She was amazed. "I thought you didn't want to see me."

"I did want to see you. And I'm sorry I didn't wait for you." He appealed to her, making a clumsy gesture with his arm in the sling.

"I'm sorry I was late." She would have to tell him sooner or later, and now was as good a time as any. "I had to go and see Ms. Davis."

"The guidance counselor? What about?"

"I'm having trouble with geometry. In fact, I need a tutor."

"Really?" He looked surprised but not disillusioned.

"Ms. Davis found one who can do it after school. But I don't want to do it then. If I did, I wouldn't be able to meet you."

He frowned as if he could see the problem.

"I told her I'd rather do it on weekends. But he can only do it after school."

"So how did you leave it?"

"I told her I had to think about it. And I said I'd let her know today."

"Well, unless she finds someone who can do it on weekends, you don't have any choice."

"I guess I don't."

"Shit," he said as if he was really disappointed.

"I'm sorry," she said, regretting more than ever that she wasn't smart.

"It's not your fault. It's the teacher's fault."

"But other people don't have trouble."

"Yeah, they do. When I took geometry, I had to help about half the class."

"You did?"

"Yeah. The whole point of geometry is teaching you how to reason," he said. "And Mr. Peters doesn't do that. He just gives you the proofs and expects you to learn them."

"He does," she agreed.

"So if you're having trouble, don't feel bad. It's because you have a lousy teacher."

"I still wish I didn't need a tutor."

He considered for a moment, and then he asked: "Can you meet me after school today?"

"Yeah. Sure."

"Okay. And don't worry. If anyone makes you late again, I'll wait for you. I'll wait all night."

"I won't be late again," she promised.

On her way back into the school she thanked God for the fact that Brian wanted to see her after all, and she prayed that everything would go well.

As they were straggling to English class she told her friends what had happened.

"So he did want to see you," Amanda said.

"Yeah. He did."

"And he wants to see you today."

"Yeah. But I have to see Ms. Davis first. I have to let her know about the tutor."

"You mean the one who can only do it after school?"

"He sounds like an old fart," Lisa said.

"She should have gotten an instructor from Fordham," Susan said, "like Jenny had."

"It's too bad this is happening," Amanda said, "just when you're starting to see Brian."

They went to Mr. Farrell's room and took their usual seats in the front row.

Mr. Farrell was an attractive man, with thick sandy hair and playful blue eyes. He had a mellifluous voice, and when he read a passage from Shakespeare you could appreciate it. He had been an actor, and he wrote poetry, which he read once a year at the bookstore down on Washington Street.

Kerry liked him, and she didn't mind sitting in the front row of his class. He was the only teacher who made her feel she had something to offer.

Today he read the "Elegy Written in a Country Churchyard," which he had assigned.

As she listened to his voice, Kerry was transported outside of herself and into a realm where she could feel the common humanity of all people.

> The boast of heraldry, the pomp of power,
> And all that beauty, all that wealth e'er gave,
> Await alike the inevitable hour.
> The paths of glory lead but to the grave.

He read through the poem, and then he asked them to explain it. He called on Steve, who mumbled that it was about the dead. Then he called on Jenny, who had nothing to add.

"Kerry," he said after calling on several other people. "I'll read a stanza, and you explain it."

> Full many a gem of purest ray serene,
> The dark unfathomed caves of ocean bear:
> Full many a flower is born to blush unseen,
> And waste its sweetness on the desert air.

She listened to him attentively without looking at her book.

"Now, what's the poet saying?" he asked her.

She cleared her throat. "He's saying there are people who have good qualities, who might be pretty, or smart, or talented, but no one ever recognizes it. So they live and die without ever realizing what they could have been."

"Exactly," he said as if he was proud of her. "You have the ability to empathize. It's a very, very special gift."

She could feel the blood tingling in her ears.

After her study period she went to see Ms. Davis. She had decided to accept the tutor since she had no choice. But before she could say anything, Mr. Davis said: "I found someone who can tutor you on weekends. I mean, I didn't find him, he came to me and offered his services."

"Who is it?" she asked, afraid to guess.

"It's Brian Donahue."

She had mixed feelings. She was glad because this showed he was really interested in her, but she was afraid he would find out how dumb she was.

"He said he knew you were having trouble with geometry, and he wanted to help you."

Kerry said nothing.

"I checked with Mr. Peters, and he said Brian would make a good tutor. So if you want him, you can have him."

"I don't know if I do," Kerry said.

Ms. Davis looked surprised. "What's the problem?"

"I'm afraid he'll find out how dumb I am."

"You're not dumb," Ms. Davis told her. "You're just having trouble with geometry."

"But what if I can't get it?"

"I think you can. But if you don't want Brian to tutor you, I'll find someone else."

"Well, I don't know."

"The retired math teacher is still available."

Kerry thought about it. And she decided that it was better to risk disillusioning Brian than not to see him. So she finally said: "I'd rather have Brian."

Ms. Davis smiled. "I know you wanted to do it after school, so you might ask him if he could do it then. I think it would be better than weekends."

"I guess it would be."

"Since he broke his arm, he can't play baseball, and he can't drive. And he needs something to do. So this could be good for both of you."

She remembered that his father wanted him to go to baseball practice, but she said nothing.

"Okay," Ms. Davis said, concluding the matter. "Work out a schedule. I think you should see him three times a week, at least until you make some progress."

"Okay," she said hopefully.

In the bathroom, while they were fixing their hair, Kerry told her friends: "I have a tutor. And guess who it is."

"Brian," Amanda said immediately.

"How did you guess?

"I could tell by looking at you."

"How did you get him?" Lisa asked.

"I told him I needed a tutor. I mean, to explain why I had to see Ms. Davis. And he went to her and volunteered."

"He likes you," Susan said.

"And you thought he didn't want to see you," Amanda said.

"You did better than Jenny," Lisa said. "You see? It pays to have trouble with geometry."

"But what if I can't get it?"

"You can. Don't worry."

They stopped at their lockers, got their books, and headed out. She parted with her friends, who were going to the door that led out to the parking lot, and she followed the corridor back to the main hall.

Outside, she found Brian waiting for her.

"Hi," he said, looking at her as if he wanted to know her reaction to what he had done.

"Hi," she said. "I saw Ms. Davis."

"So am I going to be your tutor?"

"I guess. Do you really want to do it?"

"I really do. I know I can help you."

"Would we do it on weekends?"

"We'd do it after school."

"If we do, then you won't be able to go to baseball practice."

He shook his head as if this wasn't an issue. "I went yesterday. I tried to help the pitchers. But I couldn't tell them how to throw a ball."

"Well, how do you know you can help me?"

"I helped people at geometry before."

"They were probably smarter."

"No, they weren't."

"Okay," she said, having warned him. "I just don't want you to be disappointed."

"Don't worry," he said. "I won't be disappointed."

But she couldn't help worrying, and she wondered if she had made the right decision.

"Do you feel like going for a walk?" he asked.

"Yeah. It's a nice day."

They went down the hill and turned onto the aqueduct. They passed her house and continued walking toward Dobbs Ferry.

"I live up there," he said, pointing to a modern house at the top of the ridge. It had a large window that looked out toward the river.

"You must have a good view."

"We do. I'll show it to you, but not right now. I don't want to get stuck with my mother."

She thought she saw a woman standing at the window, watching them. But when she looked back the window was empty, so it had probably just been her imagination.

They walked behind the townhouses that had been built on the site of one of Washington's headquarters. All that was left of the former estate was a low stone building, nestled between the aqueduct and an indoor pool.

They went through Dobbs Ferry, looking down into the gardens in back of the houses on Main Street. A few had already been turned and prepared for the growing season.

Then they crossed Cedar Street and followed the path behind the high school. They stopped at the campus of Mercy College, where you had an open view of the river. Here it widened into the Tappan Zee, and instead of the Palisades, there were rolling hills on the other side. In the hazy distance you could just barely see the mountains.

"Come on," she said, leading him. "I want to show you my favorite place."

They followed the path into Irvington, and soon they came to Nevis, the estate of Alexander Hamilton's son. The red brick mansion was being used by Columbia University, and there were cars in the parking lot. But in a while they would be gone.

"Look," she said, pointing toward an enormous tree. "It's a copper beech. It's a hundred and forty-three years old."

"How do you know?"

"There's a marker in front of it."

They approached the tree, whose lowest limbs had a span of about fifty feet. Its branches were still bare, but in another month its reddish brown leaves would begin to unfurl.

He studied the tree. "It still looks healthy."

"When it has leaves, it's beautiful."

She led him toward the river. They went over a rise, and then into a hollow, where you couldn't be seen by people walking along the path. "This is my place."

"I like it," he said. He looked at the tree, which gave them shelter, and then at the river, which gave them a vision.

"I come here to get away," she said, taking the risk of revealing herself.

"I understand," he said.

She sat down and leaned back against the hillside, gazing out at the dark water.

He joined her, sitting a few feet away.

He acted like he wanted to avoid having physical contact with her. And she wondered if he liked her as a girl or only as a friend.

"It's a great view," he said. "You can even see the bridge."

She followed his eyes toward the Tappan Zee Bridge, which for some reason had been built at the widest point of the river. It had a long causeway that gradually rose to a high span. It had to be high enough to let the ships pass under it.

"So you've never gone across the river," Brian said.

"No. I never have," she said.

"When I was ten, I tried to run away from home. I got halfway across the bridge before my father caught up with me."

"Where were you going?"

"As far as I could go."

"Why were you running away?"

"Because of my mother. She was always sick. She was always unhappy. And I always felt it was my fault."

"Do you still feel that way?"

"Not always. But sometimes I do. And then I want to run away," he said, staring at the bridge as if it was his evacuation route.

She felt his distress, and wanting to relieve him of it, she said: "Well, it's not your fault. Whatever is wrong with your mother, it's not your fault."

"How do you know?" he asked, turning to her.

"I just know," she said positively.

He gazed at her as if she was the only person who could make him believe that.

When she got home from school on Friday her mother was standing in the front hall, ready to go out for dinner. It was only a few minutes after six, but her mother projected the feeling that if they didn't hurry they wouldn't get a table.

"Go and get ready," her mother said.

She rushed upstairs and changed her top and fixed her hair, and then she joined her family down in the hall.

"Where are we going to eat?" her father asked.

"I want to have pizza," Bobby said.

"We had pizza last week," her mother said. "I want to have Chinese tonight."

"What do you want, Kerry?" her father asked.

"I don't care."

So they went to the Golden Wok in Ardsley.

"Let's have dumplings," Bobby said.

"We can have the shrimp dumplings," her father said. "But we can't have pork or chicken."

"I know." It was Lent, so they couldn't eat meat on Friday.

Her father ordered the dumplings, and then he asked Bobby: "How's baseball practice?"

"I don't know. I'm hitting well. But I'm having trouble with my fielding."

"Is it the grounders?"

"Yeah. I'm misjudging them."

"Well, we can work on that tomorrow."

The dumplings arrived, and for a while there wasn't much conversation.

And then her mother asked: "Did they find you a tutor?"

"Yeah. They did. I'm going to see him after school."

"Where did they get him?"

"He's a student."

"A student?"

"Yeah. The teacher recommended him."

"What's his name?"

"Brian Donahue."

"What?" Bobby said, dropping a chopstick. "You have Brian Donahue as a tutor?"

"Is that the boy you were talking about last week?" her mother asked.

"Yeah. The white knight," Bobby said.

"The boy who played basketball with a broken arm?"

"He didn't know it was broken," Kerry said.

"Have we ever met his parents?"

"I don't think so," her father said. He asked Kerry: "Do they go to our church?"

"I don't know," she said, not wanting to explain.

"Where do they live?"

"They live above the aqueduct toward Dobbs Ferry."

"If the teacher recommended him," her father said, "then he must be all right."

"How often are you going to see him?" her mother asked.

"Ms. Davis said I should see him at least three times a week."

"Where will you see him?"

"I don't know." They hadn't yet arranged a place to meet, but she imagined meeting him at her place under the copper beech. "I guess at school."

They moved on to another subject, and Kerry was relieved. For a while she had been worried that her mother wouldn't approve of Brian as her tutor. And deep down, she could almost understand why not.

FIVE

ON MONDAY AFTER school she met Brian in the hall, and they headed for Mr. Peter's room. At this point she wished he hadn't volunteered to tutor her since she was afraid she wouldn't be able to do better at geometry.

"You know," he said, breaking the silence. "My father still wants me to go to baseball practice."

"Maybe you should."

He stopped abruptly. "You don't want me to tutor you?"

"I do," she said. "But I don't want to cause a problem with your father."

"You won't. There already is a problem."

"Well, I don't want to make it worse."

"You won't," he assured her.

Now she felt even more pressure to do better.

As they went into Mr. Peter's room she was reminded of her failures there, and she was dismayed.

Brian flipped on the lights, and then he walked to the front of the classroom. He turned and faced her. "Where do you want to start?"

"I don't know." She set her book on Mr. Peter's desk and opened it. She leafed through the pages, looking for the proposition he had introduced that morning. "Let's start here."

Brian leaned over and studied the proposition.

She was conscious of his face being only a few inches from hers. She tried to keep her eyes on the book.

"Okay," he said. "You have two parallel lines, which are intersected by a third line, and you have to prove that the corresponding angles are equal."

She listened attentively.

He went to the board and drew two lines. "I'm not good at drawing, especially with my left hand, but these lines are supposed to be parallel."

She nodded, determined to follow him.

"If I intersect them with a third line," he said, drawing it, "I create some angles.

She looked at them.

"Now, what are these two angles?"

"They're supplementary."

"What does that mean?"

"It means their sum is a hundred eighty degrees."

"That's right," he said, encouraging her. And from there he led her through the proof.

"I think I can do it," she said, summoning the courage.

"Show me," he said, handing her the chalk.

She approached the board and began the proof. For a while she was able to repeat it from memory, but then she forgot what he had done.

He waited patiently.

"I don't remember what you did next."

"You don't have to remember. You can reason your way."

She looked at the lines and angles. She went to the point where she had forgotten what he had done next, and reasoning her way, she completed the proof.

"You did it," he said, grinning.

He had made her feel she wasn't so dumb after all, and she wanted to show him how grateful she was, but she didn't know how, so she just thanked him.

She was sitting on the back steps, watching her father and Bobby play catch. The dinner was ready, and all they had to do was heat it up when her mother got home, so she had time to sit there and reflect.

When she had gotten home she had gone up to her room, sat at her desk, and repeated the proof, just to see if she could do it by herself. And she had done it with no problem. But she didn't know if she could do it for Mr. Peters, in front of everyone.

"We're going to miss him," Bobby said, waiting for his father to throw the ball.

"You don't have any other pitchers?"

"We do, but no one like him."

"Then you'll have to win on your hitting. And on your fielding," his father said, slinging a grounder.

Bobby caught it, even though it took a wicked bounce, and he held it up in triumph.

"Good get," his father said.

"Do you think I could be a pitcher?"

"Maybe. But you'd really have to work at it."

"Let me try a fastball."

"Okay. Go ahead."

Bobby took a stance like a pitcher, wound up, and hurled the ball as hard as he could.

His father caught it, saying: "Not bad."

"Could you have hit that?'

"I don't know. But I wouldn't have swung at it," his father added. "It was low and inside."

"Let me try again."

"Not now. If you want to pitch to me, I'll have to buy a catcher's mitt."

"You mean I'm that fast?"

"You're fast enough for me to feel it."

"Will you buy a mitt tomorrow?"

"We'll see," his father said.

Listening to them, Kerry wondered if Brian could have helped the pitchers, and she worried that his father would give him a hard time for not going to baseball practice.

The next day, as she went into Mr. Peter's room for geometry class, she felt like she was about to take a final exam.

She took her usual seat in the front row, with Amanda on her left and Lisa on her right. She got out her notebook and her pen. And she took a deep breath.

Mr. Peters was standing at the board, waiting for the boys in the last row to settle down.

For once she was anxious to begin the class.

"Okay," Mr. Peters said finally. "Today we're going prove the proposition that the sum of the angles of a triangle is equal to one hundred eighty degrees."

Kerry was able to follow him for a while, but then she got lost, and she wondered if she would ever be good at geometry.

Mr. Peters turned and faced the class. "Can anyone tell me what to do next?"

As usual she bent her head over her notebook.

"Jason? Can you tell me?"

Jason was one of the boys in the last row, and he promptly replied: "No. I can't."

"I thought you always knew what to do next," Steve said.

"I do with a girl, but not with geometry."

"Okay, okay," Mr. Peters said, cutting them off. "Lisa, can you help us?"

"Well, since the interior and the exterior angles are on a straight line," Lisa said, "their sum is equal to a hundred eighty degrees."

"Right." He completed the proof and set down his chalk. "Now, let's review the proposition we proved yesterday."

Kerry perked up.

"Who wants to try it?"

On a sudden impulse she raised her hand. She had never raised her hand before, and she knew that everyone was surprised, especially Mr. Peters.

"Kerry?" he said as if she might be someone else. "You want to try it?"

"Yeah," she said, her hand wavering.

"Okay. Come on."

She got up from her desk, already wishing she hadn't raised her hand. She now had doubts that she could do it.

"State the proposition."

She picked up the chalk and said: "If two parallel lines are intersected by a third line, then the corresponding angles are equal."

"Right. Go ahead."

She drew the lines, and then she began the proof. Instead of trying to remember it, she reasoned her way, and she went slowly, deliberately.

She paused to think about the next step.

"Are you stuck?" Mr. Peters asked impatiently.

"Give her a chance," Amanda said.

"Yeah. Let her think," Lisa said.

"She can do it," Susan said.

Encouraged by her friends, she figured out the step, and she completed the proof.

"Right," Mr. Peters said as if he couldn't believe it.

She went back to her desk feeling proud and happy, knowing she had made a breakthrough. And when she sat down Amanda gave her a pat on the arm.

With her eyes closed, she thanked God.

They were standing around after lunch, talking.

She spotted Brian coming their way, along with Mark. She waited until he got near enough, and then she burst out: "Hey, I did it. I proved the proposition in class."

"You did?" He looked happy but not surprised.

"Yeah. I did." She felt like hugging him.

"She did it perfectly," Lisa said.

"She surprised the hell out of Mr. Peters," Amanda said.

"She sure did," Susan said.

"Well, that shows you can do it," Brian said.

"It also shows you're a good teacher," Kerry said.

"He is," Mark said. "He taught me how to do a hook shot."

"No, I didn't. You already knew how to do one."

"I might have known how, but I couldn't get one into the basket until you helped me."

Brian shrugged as if it was nothing.

"Why don't you join us after school?" Amanda suggested.

"Oh, I don't know," Brian said, hesitating.

Seeing his reluctance, Kerry said: "We have to work on the new proposition. I didn't get it."

"I didn't either," Susan said.

"Which one was that?" Mark asked.

"The one where you have to prove that the sum of the angles of a triangle is equal to a hundred eighty degrees."

"That's easy. You just add them."

"You can't add them. You don't know what they are."

"Well, I guess I didn't get that one either.'

"So maybe we should all meet with Brian and work on it."

"Maybe we should leave them alone," Amanda said, backing away from her suggestion.

At that moment the bell rang.

That evening, while she was helping her father cook dinner, he asked her about geometry.

She had planned to tell him about her success, but he and Bobby had been so busy playing catch in the backyard that she hadn't yet had an opportunity. And now she told him how she had proven the theorem in class, in front of everyone.

"That's great," he said. "Did it help having a tutor?"

"Oh, yeah. He taught me how to reason, instead of just remembering the proof."

Her father wiped his hands on the long striped apron he wore while cooking, and he came to her and gave her a full hug, saying: "I love you. And it's not because you're doing better in geometry, it's because you're Kerry."

"I love you," she said, pressing her face against the apron.

They were unwinding from the hug when the phone rang. It was her mother, calling to tell them she would be late.

Kerry was disappointed since she wanted to tell her mother about her success, and now she would have to wait longer.

While they ate dinner her father and her brother talked about baseball.

"Do you think my pitches are fast enough?" Bobby asked.

"I could feel them," his father said, "even with a catcher's mitt."

"Could you have hit them?"

"I don't know. But I wouldn't have swung at most of them."

"You mean I have to control them better."

"Yeah. You do. Control is more important than speed. If you can put your pitches exactly where you want them, you can get the batters out."

"How can I learn to control them?"

"You could practice throwing into a barrel."

"Where can we get a barrel?"

Her father thought. "We can get one from a nursery."

"Can we go tomorrow?"

"We'll see."

They ate in silence for a while, and then Bobby asked: "Did you see Brian today?"

"Yeah," she said, though she felt it was none of her brother's business.

"Do you see him after school every day?"

"Yeah," she said, shrugging.

"You should bring him here," Bobby said, "so he could help me with my pitching."

"He couldn't help you with a broken arm. He couldn't show you how to throw."

"He could watch me and give me pointers."

"He's helping Kerry," her father said. "She has the first call on his time."

"Well, I just thought that when they're done with geometry, they could drop by here."

"They might have other things they want to do."

Kerry said nothing. She had only begun to imagine doing other things with Brian, and she wasn't ready to find out what her father might have had in mind.

She was in her room, studying geometry. She was working on the new proposition, reasoning her way through it, when she heard her mother climbing the stairs.

"Hi," her mother said from the doorway.

"Hi," she said.

"I'm sorry I couldn't join you for dinner, but we had a crisis on the deal."

"That's okay. I understand."

"How are you doing?"

"I'm doing better at geometry. I proved a proposition in class today."

"You did? That's great," her mother said, looking pleased.

"Brian is a good tutor."

"Well, I'm glad it worked out."

Her mother left to go and change out of her work clothes, leaving the impression that since Brian was a good tutor, there was nothing to worry about.

The next day, when they left the school after the tutoring session, Brian said: "Let's go on the aqueduct."

"Okay," she said happily.

It was a sunny day, and as they walked toward Five Corners, she noticed that the forsythia was about to bloom. Its buds were swelling and faintly yellow.

They turned onto the aqueduct and headed north. They hiked as far as her place near the copper beech, and they settled down there. In the afternoon sunlight the river was blue, with flecks of silver.

"When I can drive again," Brian said, gazing at the bridge, "we can go across the river and up to Bear Mountain. We can get on the Appalachian Trail."

"Do you still feel like running away?"

"Sometimes I do. Sometimes I can't take any more."

"Is your father giving you a hard time for not going to baseball practice?"

Brian nodded. "Yeah. He is."

"But if you can't help the pitchers, why should you go?"

"He just thinks I should go."

"Are sports that important to him?"

"They're his whole life. He was a star in high school," Brian told her. "He went to college on an athletic scholarship. When he graduated, he got a contract with the Boston Red Sox. He played for one of their farm teams, and if he hadn't quit, he would have played in the big leagues."

"Why did he quit?"

"Because of my mother. If you play pro, you're on the road half the time. But she wanted him at home more, and when she got pregnant, she wanted him at home all the time. So he quit playing and became a sportswriter."

"Does he expect you to play pro?"

"Oh, yeah. He expects me to play in the big leagues."

"Do you want to be an athlete?"

"No. I don't. I want to be a psychologist. But he won't accept that. And I don't want to fight with him because when I do, it upsets my mother. So I keep doing what he wants."

"Well, I don't care what you do. I want you to be happy."

"I am, with you," he said, turning to her. "And you know what? I'm glad I broke my arm. I mean, if I hadn't, I wouldn't have met you, I wouldn't be here with you."

The way he looked at her made her feel she had finally found something she was good at.

On Friday, while they were sitting in the cafeteria, Amanda asked: "Are you going to meet Brian today after school?"

"Yeah," she said. "But not for tutoring."

"Then why don't you join us."

"I'll ask him and see what he wants to do."

"You don't ask boys what they want to do," Lisa said. "You tell them what *you* want to do."

"If you don't tell them," Susan said, "you'll end up doing what they want to do."

"And they always want to get into your pants," Amanda said.

Kerry said nothing. So far there wasn't any evidence that Brian wanted to do that with her.

"Just tell him you want him to join your friends," Lisa said.

"Tell him," Susan said, "that since he's been seeing you every day after school, we hardly see you anymore."

"Okay," she said, imagining what it would be like being in Kevin's car with a boyfriend.

When she found Brian in the hall she told him: "My friends want us to join them after school. Mark will be with them."

"Where are they going?"

"I don't know. They usually go over to Central Avenue."

"Do you want go with them?"

"Yeah. I mean, if you do."

"So let's go with them."

After school Kerry and her friends went from their lockers to the parking lot, where Kevin was standing by his car.

"You should open the trunk," Amanda told him, "so we can put our books in it."

He did as she said, and when he took Jerry's backpack he said: "That weighs a ton. What the hell have you got in it?"

"Bars of gold," Jerry said.

"Yeah, don't you wish."

"It's his rock collection," Lisa said.

"I thought he kept the rocks in his head."

"I used to," Jerry said. "But I had to make room for all the shit the teachers give us."

At that moment Brian approached, walking with Mark.

"Give me your things," Kevin told them.

"Our things?" Mark asked.

Susan giggled. "Don't give him that."

"Don't worry. I won't."

Brian looked at the car and said: "There isn't room for eight people."

"Yeah, there is," Amanda said.

"We can sit on your laps," Susan said.

"Except for Amanda," Lisa pointed out.

"If she tells me where to go," Kevin said with a straight face, "I can drive with Amanda in my lap."

"I know you can," Jerry said. "But I want to get out of the parking lot."

"Well, I don't know," Brian said, looking skeptical. "With my cast it wouldn't be comfortable sitting on my lap."

"He has a point," Amanda said. "Susan, why don't you and Mark sit in front with us."

"It's against the law to have four in the front," Lisa said.

"We won't get caught," Kevin said. "The cops have more important things to look for."

So four of them sat in front.

In back, Lisa sat on Jerry's lap, and Kerry sat between them and Brian. She wouldn't have minded sitting on his lap even if it wasn't comfortable. In fact, she would have preferred that. But it might not have been good for his arm, and at least she was sitting next to him, with her body touching his.

"Are we all in?" Kevin asked.

"Yeah, we're all in," Susan said.

"I'm under," Jerry said.

The car lurched forward with a squeal of rubber.

"That's the way," Mark said.

"It's the way to crush me," Jerry said.

"Oh, I don't weigh that much," Lisa said.

"You do at liftoff."

They went out of the parking lot, turning left, and Kerry was thrown against Brian.

He leaned away from her.

"I'm sorry," she said.

"That's okay."

"I didn't hurt your arm, did I?"

"No. You didn't."

She sensed it wasn't his arm that made him uneasy. It was something else. She wondered if it was being so close to her, without being able to get away. And she wondered if he only liked her as a friend.

"Where are we going?" Kevin asked.

"You should know," Mark said. "You're driving."

"Let's go over to Central Avenue," Susan said.

"Oh, that's so unsophisticated," Lisa said.

"We're not going to Bloomingdale's," Jerry said. "That gives me a headache."

"I'm for Central Avenue," Mark said.

"There's nothing on Central Avenue," Lisa said.

"There's McDonald's."

"I'm not hungry."

"I am. I could use some fries."

"So could I," Kevin said. "Some fries and a Coke."

"Well, they do have good fries," Lisa admitted.

"Then let's go there," Amanda said.

They turned off Farragut and onto Ravensdale Road. They hit a bump going up the bridge over the Saw Mill River Parkway, and everyone bounced.

"I'm going to sue you," Lisa said, holding her hand on the top of her head, which had hit the roof. "I'm going to sue you for a million dollars."

"Talk to my attorney," Kevin said.

"Are you insured for that much?" Jerry asked.

"Yeah. I am. So if you win and collect the money, you can split it with me."

"You can split it with all of us," Amanda said.

"We could buy some clothes," Lisa said.

"We could have a party," Susan said.

Kerry said nothing.

They went up the steep hill on Jackson and then around a left curve, and Kerry was thrown against Brian again.

Again, he leaned away from her.

"I'm sorry," she said.

"That's okay."

When they arrived at McDonald's they all went in and lined up to place their orders.

"What are you going to have?" Brian asked her.

"I don't know. I guess I'll have some fries and a Coke."

He ordered for both of them and paid for her, even though she had her money out. It was the first time a boy had treated her.

"Are we going to eat here?" Susan asked.

"No, this place is a dump," Lisa said.

"We can eat in the car," Amanda said.

So they all trooped out.

They got back into the car and headed up Central Avenue.

Kevin had to drive, and Jerry was in no position to eat, so their girls fed them, slipping fries into their mouths and holding drinks for them to sip.

Brian had a problem since he couldn't use his right arm, and after trying to manage by himself he let Kerry feed him.

By the time they had finished he no longer seemed so uneasy.

Kerry decided that he had been uneasy since he wasn't used to being in a group like this.

"Where are we going?" Kevin asked.

"To White Plains," Lisa said.

"To Tarrytown," Susan said.

"Well, make a decision. I have to go one way or the other."

"Go left," Brian said.

Responding to his authority, Kevin turned left, and Kerry was thrown against Brian again.

And this time he didn't lean away from her.

When she got home she looked through the mail and found an envelope with Ms. Davis's name on it. She couldn't open it since it wasn't addressed to her, but she guessed what was in it, and she left it on top so her mother would see it.

Her father saw it first. He came in the back door, and after giving her a hug he picked up the mail from the counter. "Hey, who's Ms. Davis?"

"She's the guidance counselor."

"Well, let's see what she has to say," her father said, opening the letter.

Kerry waited while he read it.

"She says you're doing better in geometry."

"I am doing better."

"That's great. We have to show this to your mother." He left the letter on the counter and went upstairs to change his clothes.

She was sitting on the back steps, watching her brother throw pitches to her father, when her mother got home, evidently having made the six-twenty train. She heard her mother in the kitchen, and she waited anxiously for her to come out.

The door opened.

Holding the letter, her mother said: "So you're doing better at geometry."

"Yeah. I am. Thanks to Brian."

"Well, then you should keep seeing him."

"I will," she said, trying to make it sound like an obligation.

In church on Sunday she gave thanks for having Brian as her tutor, and after saying her usual prayers for people she prayed for him. She prayed that his arm would be all right, but she went further and asked God to make him happy.

SIX

THE FOLLOWING FRIDAY she and Brian joined her friends and rode around with them. This time he said that if she didn't mind sitting on his lap, it was all right with him. So she sat on his lap, with the cast between them.

When they brought her home Brian got out with her, and she led him around to the backyard where she knew her father and her brother would be playing catch.

At the sight of Brian her brother gaped.

Her father, who had been about to throw the ball back to Bobby, stopped and turned.

"Dad," she said, "this is Brian."

"Hi, Brian," her father said with a friendly smile. He chucked the ball into his mitt and stepped toward Brian, extending his hand.

"I'm glad to meet you," Brian said, shaking with his left hand.

"I want to thank you for helping Kerry."

Brian shrugged as if it was nothing.

Bobby approached them.

"Brian," Kerry said, "this is my brother Bobby."

"Hi, Bobby."

"Hi," her brother managed to say. He seemed overwhelmed by the fact that he was actually meeting Brian Donahue.

"Bobby plays on the CYO team," her father said.

"What position?" Brian asked.

"Second base," Bobby said.

"But now he wants to be a pitcher."

"You do? Really?"

"Yeah," Bobby said hopefully.

"He has a fastball, but he has to learn how to control it."

Brian nodded. "Control is everything."

"What's your favorite team in the majors?" Bobby asked as if this was vital.

"The Mets, of course."

"That's my team," Bobby said, delighted. "My Dad's team is the Yankees. But he can't help it. He's from the Bronx."

"I cheer for the Mets," his father said, "except when they're playing the Yankees."

"Do you think they have a chance to win?"

"I think they do. It'll all depend on their pitching."

Kerry and her father listened while the boys analyzed the Mets' strengths and weaknesses, discussing Hernandez and Gooden and Strawberry and Carter and Knight and Dykstra and Fernandez. She recognized the names from watching the Mets on television with her father and her brother, but if they had come up out of context, she might not have known if they were Mets or Yankees since it didn't make any difference to her.

Her father sat down next to her on the back steps, staying out of the conversation.

The boys were talking about the bull pen when her mother appeared at the back door. She was wearing a navy blue suit.

"Hi, Mom," Kerry said through the screen. "Come out and meet Brian."

Her mother came out and stood on the porch.

"Mom, this is Brian."

"Hi, Brian," her mother said.

"I'm glad to meet you," Brian said.

"We appreciate what you're doing for Kerry."

Again, Brian shrugged as if it was nothing.

Her mother studied him, and then she glanced at her watch. "Well, we better get ready."

"Can Brian come with us?" Bobby asked.

"We're going out for dinner," her father said. "Would you like to join us?"

Brian looked at her mother, whose face didn't welcome him.

"Thanks. I'd like to, but I have to go home and eat with my parents."

"Maybe some other time."

"Yeah. Maybe."

"I'm going to change," her mother said to everyone except Brian, "and I expect you to be ready when I come back."

"I better go," Brian said.

Kerry got up and walked with him to the gate that led to the aqueduct. "My mother makes such a big deal about going out for dinner on Friday since it's about the only time she eats with us. And she always has to get to the restaurant before the crowd. She hates having to wait for a table."

"I understand."

When they reached the gate they gazed at each other in silence.

"Well, I'll see you," he said finally.

"Okay," she said, believing he meant it but wishing he had told her when.

"I like him," her father said as they drove to Sam's.

"I wish he could have come with us," Bobby said.

Kerry said nothing. She was annoyed at her mother for not welcoming him to join them.

"I hope you're not getting involved with him," her mother said after a silence.

"Why shouldn't I get involved with him?"

"I think there's something wrong with him. I mean, anyone who would keep playing basketball with a broken arm—"

"He didn't know it was broken."

"But he must have been in terrible pain."

"People have different thresholds for pain," her father said.

"Well, maybe he didn't feel it," her mother said, "because he takes drugs."

"He doesn't take drugs."

"How do you know? From what I heard, half the kids in your high school take drugs."

"None of my friends do, and Brian doesn't."

"He knew the team was depending on him," Bobby said, "so he ignored the pain. And he won the championship for us."

"Maybe he was trying to prove something," her mother said, not letting go of it.

"He wasn't trying to prove anything," Kerry said.

"We don't know anything about his parents. Maybe it has to do with them."

She remembered how his father had examined his injury and had shaken his head as if it was nothing, and she could see what her mother might be driving at, but she wasn't going to give her mother any ammunition.

"I think he was just trying to win the game," her father said.

"I wonder," her mother said.

She was gazing out the window at Amanda's house, thinking about what her mother had said.

"Kerry," Susan called to her.

She turned her head from the window. "Yeah?"

"We're having a party at Lisa's tonight, and I could ask Mark to bring Brian."

She hesitated. "I don't know if my mother will let me go out with him."

"Why wouldn't she let you go out with him?" Amanda asked.

"She thinks there's something wrong with him."

"If there's something wrong with Brian," Susan said, "then the other boys are hopeless cases."

"Don't tell her you're going out with him," Lisa said. "Just tell her you're going to a party."

"What if she found out that Brian was there?"

"How would she find out?"

"I don't know. She might ask me."

"Then tell her Brian's going to be there."

"If I do, she might not let me go."

"If she doesn't, then you can argue with her."

"I don't like to argue with my mother."

"Well, at times you have to. Mothers aren't always right."

"Brian's your tutor, and he's helping you," Amanda said. "So how can your mother have a problem with him?"

"I don't know," Kerry said, beginning to feel like arguing with her mother.

"Should I call Mark and ask him to bring Brian to the party?" Susan asked her.

"Yeah," she said, emboldened by them.

Susan called Mark.

A while later Mark called back and said that he would bring Brian. The only thing was, Brian had to do an errand for his mother, so they would be a little late.

Kerry didn't mind. It would give her time to calm herself before he arrived.

When she got home she found her parents in the kitchen. Her father was standing at the counter, preparing a steak for the grill, and her mother was sitting at the table, drinking white wine.

She took a deep breath and then told them: "My friends are having a party at Lisa's. Brian will be there. Can I go?"

"I don't want you to get involved with him," her mother said.

"There's nothing wrong with him," Kerry insisted.

"He's done a good job of helping Kerry," her father said.

"It's one thing to have him as a tutor," her mother said. "It's another thing to have him as a boyfriend."

"He's not my boyfriend," Kerry said honestly.

"He's not now, but he could become your boyfriend."

"So what if that happened?" her father asked. "You don't think she could handle it?"

"She has no experience with boyfriends," her mother said, "and I don't want her to begin with a boy who plays basketball with a broken arm."

"Well, I think we should let her go to the party. She's not going out on a date with him. They'll be with other people."

"All right," her mother said, yielding.

Kerry raced upstairs and took a shower, washing her hair. It dried quickly, and it fell into place when she shook her head. It wasn't a problem anymore.

She decided to wear her gray leggings and her new pink sweater, wanting to look as sexy as possible. And when she was dressed she examined herself in the full-length mirror on the bathroom door. At least she didn't have a bad body.

She bounced downstairs and strolled into the kitchen.

"You look terrific," her father said.

"That's a pretty sweater," her mother said.

They acted like they had been discussing her, but they said nothing more about Brian.

She set the table, and while they ate she listened to the conversation. But she was thinking about Brian, hoping he liked her as a girl.

"Have a good time," her father said as she was leaving.

"Is someone going to bring you home?" her mother asked.

"Mark is," she said, though she didn't know.

"Well, don't walk home on the aqueduct."

"Don't worry. I won't."

When she arrived at Lisa's they were watching a basketball game. She knew it was the playoffs, and she assumed that when Brian and Mark got there they would want to watch it too. So she sat down on the floor, next to Amanda.

"This is boring," Lisa said.

"No, it's not," Kevin said. "You don't understand it."

"What's to understand? It's just a lot of big black guys running back and forth, dunking a ball into a basket."

"You're missing the subtleties."

"I guess I am. When did Mark say they'd be here?'

"Around seventy-thirty."

"Well, then we have time to make something. That would be more interesting."

"I agree," Amanda said, rousing herself.

The girls went into the kitchen, leaving Kevin and Jerry in front of the television.

"What should we make?" Lisa asked.

"Let's make brownies," Amanda said. "Do you remember your recipe, Kerry?"

"I think so," Kerry said. She began to name the ingredients, and Lisa checked to see if they had them, opening the doors of the cabinets.

"It looks like we have everything," Lisa said.

So they made brownies.

Kerry was taking the pan out of the oven when she heard Brian and Mark arrive. She could feel her heart thumping with excitement. She was finally going to see him at night.

"Hey, that smells good," Mark said, coming into the kitchen.

Brian was a few steps behind him. He wore a sweatshirt, with one sleeve dangling.

"These are Kerry's famous brownies," Amanda said.

"They're the best," Susan said.

"Then let's have some," Mark said.

"No. Not yet," Lisa said. "We have to let them cool for a while."

"Hi," Brian said, approaching Kerry. "I wish I could have gotten here sooner."

"That's okay."

"You really look pretty."

She felt the blood rush to her cheeks.

"Come on," Mark said. "We have to watch the game."

"Why do we have to?" Susan asked.

"Because it's the playoffs."

"It's boring," Lisa said.

"If they want to watch it," Amanda said, "then we'll go and find some other guys."

"We'll go to Central Avenue," Susan said.

"You better not," Mark said.

"You can't stop us."

"Yes, I can." Mark lunged for Susan.

She dodged him, going around Brian, and then fleeing out of the kitchen.

Mark pursued her.

"You don't want to watch the game, do you?" Amanda said to Brian.

"No," he said. "I've had enough basketball for this season."

"Then you can help us get the guys away from the game."

A scream, which resolved into laughter, came from the living room. It sounded like Mark had caught Susan.

"I don't think we'll need help with that one," Lisa said.

"Let's put on some music," Amanda said.

They went into the family room, and Lisa put on some tapes that Susan had brought.

"Turn that down," Jerry said.

Ignoring him, Amanda and Susan started dancing.

Brian stood and watched them.

Kerry swayed to the rhythm of the music, hoping he would get the idea.

"You want to dance?" he finally asked.

"Yeah. I mean, if you want to."

When they began he was tentative and stiff. He obviously wasn't used to dancing. And he followed her as if he was trying to learn from her.

By now Kevin and Jerry had abandoned the game and were dancing with Amanda and Lisa. Mark and Susan had joined them. And being there with a boy she liked, with a boy who seemed to like her, Kerry finally felt she belonged.

When Susan put on some slow music Brian couldn't put his right arm around her, and the cast got in the way. It hung between them, just below her breasts. But he put his left arm around her, and with both her arms around him, she snuggled against him, closing her eyes and thanking God for making her so happy.

It was after eleven when she got home.

Her parents were in the family room, reading. They looked like they were waiting up for her.

"Did you have a good time?" her father asked.

"Yeah. I did," she said, smiling.

"It's a little late," her mother observed.

"My friends are still there."

"Well, their parents can let them do whatever they want, but we have limits."

"Let's not talk about that tonight," her father said.

"Okay," her mother said. "We'll talk about it tomorrow."

She kissed them goodnight and headed upstairs. But hearing their voices, she stopped and listened from the landing.

"I'd rather see her come home late than early," her father said. "You should have seen her face the last time she came home from a party."

"I know," her mother said, not without sympathy.

"And it's not that late."

"The point is, unless she has a limit she might come home at two the next time."

"Oh, I don't think she would."

"I don't either. But I know what happens. The boy wants to stay out all night, and if you have to be home by a certain hour, you have an excuse."

"You're right about boys," her father said. "They go as far as girls let them. But Brian doesn't seem like the kind of boy who would take advantage of a girl."

"He doesn't. But I don't want her to get involved with him. I think he has problems."

"Why do you think that?"

"Boys who are heroes always have problems. And girls who fall in love with them always get hurt."

There was a silence.

"So we'll give her limits," her father finally said.

They stopped talking, and expecting them to come to bed, she scampered the rest of the way upstairs and went into her room.

On Monday, while they were standing around in the hall at school, she told her friends: "My mother set a limit. When I go out at night, I have to be home by eleven."

"Don't worry," Amanda said. "After a while she'll let you stay out later."

"She will," Susan said. "When I started going out with Mark, I had to be home by eleven."

"What time do you have to be home now?"

"By twelve," Susan said.

"We all have to be home by twelve," Amanda said.

"Our mothers got together," Lisa said. "We were playing them off against each other."

"I told my mother," Susan said, "that Lisa could stay out until one, and she told her mother that I could stay out until one."

"It almost worked," Lisa said. "But then my mother called hers, and they agreed on twelve."

"Well, I wish I could stay out until twelve," Kerry said.

"Your mother will let you," Amanda assured her. "Just give her time."

Kerry hoped that Amanda was right. She had accepted the limit without arguing since she felt lucky that her mother was letting her go out with Brian. But she already felt constrained by it, though she couldn't have explained why.

During that week Brian asked if she could go out with him on Saturday night, and happily she said yes. It was the first time he had asked her out on a date.

Since he was vague about what they were going to do, she suggested that they join her friends, who were having a party at Lisa's again. And he agreed as if he had been hoping to do something like that.

Instead of meeting her at the party, he came and got her after having dinner with his parents. She and her mother were in the kitchen, cleaning up, when the doorbell rang.

Before she could even dry her hands she heard Bobby run to the door and open it.

"Have a good time," her mother said. "And remember, we expect you home by eleven."

She found Brian in the family room, talking about the Mets with her brother while her father stayed out of the conversation.

"Hi," Brian said, gazing at her.

"Hi," she said, hoping she looked all right.

"You really look pretty."

"She does," her father agreed heartily.

Bobby turned away in disgust.

"Well, have a good time," her father said. He didn't remind her that they expected her home by eleven. He didn't have to.

When they arrived at the party Brian stayed with her instead of joining the other boys, who were watching a basketball game. He talked with her and her friends in the kitchen. And when they put on some music he danced with her.

She hadn't told him about the limit since she hadn't wanted to put a damper on the evening, and she was having such a good time, she forgot about it. But later, while they were dancing to a slow one, holding each other as closely as possible with the cast between them, she suddenly remembered to check her watch.

"I have to go," she told him sadly.

"What time is it?"

"It's quarter to eleven."

"What time do you have to be home?"

"By eleven."

He frowned. "You didn't have to be home by eleven last week."

"I do now. My mother set a limit."

"She did? Why?"

"She thinks I need one."

"You mean with me?"

"With anyone," she said, not wanting him to feel that he was being discriminated against.

"Do you want to stay out later?"

"Yeah. But I can't."

"Okay," he said, looking dejected.

They left the party and headed toward the aqueduct.

"I really don't want to go home," she said, trying to reassure him.

Brian said nothing.

She didn't know what else to say.

They arrived at her house with a minute to spare. They stopped at the foot of the back steps.

"Do you like me?" he asked as if his life depended on it.

"Yeah. I do." She went further, saying: "I love you."

But he looked as if he didn't believe it.

So she proved it the only way she could. She leaned toward him and kissed him, putting her whole heart into it.

And he responded.

SEVEN

NOW THAT THEY had kissed, they couldn't get enough of it. They kissed whenever they had an opportunity. They kissed behind the lockers in school, they kissed in Mr. Peters' room, they kissed on the aqueduct, and they kissed at their place near the copper beech. Over and over, she proved she loved him, and Brian confirmed that he loved her.

She didn't see him on Good Friday since she went with her father and her brother to the afternoon service, where the priest and the readers did the passion from the gospel of St. John. Her mother had said she would try to make it but called at the last moment to tell them to go ahead without her.

The next evening, after some discussion of the fact that it was Holy Saturday, her parents let her go to the party at Lisa's, yielding to her arguments that her friends were all going.

But they reminded her of the limit and of the fact that the next day was Easter.

At the party they kissed while they were dancing. They kissed on the sofa. And they went so deeply into kissing, they almost forgot that she had to be home by eleven.

When she did get home, just in time, she decided to try to extend the limit. She found her parents in the family room, reading. And facing them, she said: "My friends can all stay out until twelve. So why can't I?"

"Because we want you home by eleven," her mother said.

"That's not a reason."

"Yes, it is."

"But if they can all stay out until twelve—"

"I don't care what they can do."

"You say I should keep trying to catch up, but now with this limit you're holding me back."

"You mean socially."

"Yeah. Do you want me to be socially retarded?"

"No. We don't. But making you get home by eleven won't hold you back."

"Then why do it?"

"What do you mean?"

"If it won't hold me back," Kerry argued, "why make me get home by eleven?"

Looking at her father, her mother said: "I think we have another lawyer in the family."

"I think we do," her father said, smiling.

She waited, hoping they would come around.

"Okay, okay. You can stay out until twelve. But if you're one minute late," her mother warned her, "you'll be grounded. Is that clear?"

She nodded. "Yeah."

A week passed, and on Monday of the following week Brian's cast was taken off. His arm was shriveled after being encased for six weeks, but other than that it seemed all right. Just to make sure, his father sent him to a doctor at Lenox Hill Hospital, which had a clinic for sports medicine, and the next morning Brian found her in the hall and took her aside.

"What did the doctor say?" she asked anxiously.

"He said I not only broke my arm, I also tore some ligaments. He said I must have done that when I kept playing. And that was worse than breaking it. So I need therapy."

"Where will you get it?"

"At a sports clinic in Scarsdale."

"How often will you have to go there?"

"Twice a week," he said. "I have appointments for Thursdays and Saturdays."

"If you want to go more often, you don't have to tutor me."

"The doctor said twice a week is enough."

"Well, I don't want to interfere with your therapy."

"Don't worry. You won't."

She still worried. "Will your arm be all right after the therapy?"

"He said it will. And he should know. He's the doctor for the Mets."

She was relieved for him, remembering how worried he had been. But at the same time she knew that when his arm got better his father would want him to play baseball.

That day, after their tutoring session, she brought him home, and while they were sitting in the kitchen, having cookies and milk, her brother barged in.

"Hi, Bobby," Brian said. "How's your fastball?"

"It's getting better." Emboldened, Bobby asked: "Do you want to see it?'

"Sure," Brian said without hesitation.

Bobby gave him the catcher's mitt, and they all went out to the backyard.

She sat on the steps to watch them.

Her brother wound up and hurled the ball, losing his balance as he followed through.

Brian had to lunge to get it.

"Sorry," Bobby said.

"That's okay. You have to control it. Now, try again with a little less speed."

Bobby tried again.

"That's better. Speed is important, but control is even more important. You should be able to put the ball wherever you want to. Now, try again."

She watched Brian help her brother with baseball, just as he had helped her with geometry.

They were still at it when her father got home.

"Brian's helping me," Bobby told him.

"I can see that," her father said, standing on the lawn. "Brian, you're nice to help him, but I hope you're not straining your arm."

"I'm not. He's doing all the work."

"Watch," Bobby said, ready to wind up. He was standing the way Brian had shown him.

"Put it here," Brian said, squatting like a catcher.

Bobby pitched the ball right into the mitt.

"That's the way."

"I could have thrown it faster."

"That was fast enough."

"Could you have hit that?" Bobby asked his father.

"I don't know. But I would have had to swing at it. It was in the groove."

Bobby looked gratified.

"I'll be right back," her father said.

When he came back he was in jeans and a sweatshirt, and he advised Brian to take a break. So Brian sat down next to her, and they watched her father throw grounders to Bobby.

Then the phone rang.

"I'll get it," Kerry said, jumping up. She ran into the kitchen.

It was her mother, calling to say she had to work late.

Kerry wasn't disappointed. She saw an opportunity for her father to get to know Brian.

She went back out, saying: "That was Mom. She has to work late."

"Can Brian stay for dinner?" Bobby asked as if he had read her mind.

"Would you like to?" her father asked Brian.

"Well—" He looked at her for guidance.

She nodded eagerly.

"Yeah. Sure."

She made spaghetti and meatballs with Brian's help. And since it was now warm enough, they ate outside at the picnic table. They slurped down noodles while Brian and Bobby discussed Hernandez and Gooden and Strawberry.

When it was time for Brian to leave she walked slowly with him to the gate.

"I like your father," Brian said.

"He likes you. And you were so nice to help Bobby."

Brian shrugged as if it was nothing.

She wanted him to know how much she loved him, so rising on her toes and putting her arms around him, she gave him a very special kiss.

On Wednesday she brought him home after their tutoring session. He helped Bobby more with his fastball, and when her father took over he sat down next to her.

Her father had just thrown a grounder to Bobby when the back door opened and her mother came out, still dressed for work.

"Hello, Mrs. McGrath," Brian said, getting up.

"Hello, Brian," her mother said, almost being friendly.

"No more," her father said to Bobby.

"One more grounder."

"Okay. But only one more."

"I better go," Brian said.

"Yeah," she said, knowing it would be a mistake to ask if Brian could stay for dinner.

They walked to the gate.

"I'll see you tomorrow," Brian said.

"Okay." She kissed him goodbye and watched him go.

When he looked back she waved to him.

She was going into the house when she heard her parents talking in the kitchen. She stopped on the back porch to listen.

"He's a good boy," her father said.

"I think she's seeing too much of him," her mother said.

"I don't see anything wrong with it. He's helping her with geometry, and he's helping Bobby with pitching."

"You don't see what's happening."

"What's happening?"

"She's getting involved with him," her mother said. "She's in love with him."

"So she's in love with him. Weren't you in love at her age?"

"I was. That's how I know what can happen to her."

"Well, we can't protect her from everything. We have to let her live and learn."

"She has her whole life ahead of her. She doesn't have to live and learn everything now."

"I know she doesn't," her father said. "But I don't think this boy will hurt her."

"Maybe he won't. But I think we should put a limit on how many times a week she can see him."

"How could we do that? She sees him every day at school."

"I'm not worried about that. I'm worried about her seeing him every day after school."

"Let's think about it. Okay?"

"Okay. But let's not wait too long before we do something about it."

Assuming they were done talking about it, Kerry went into the kitchen and joined them, ready to argue with her mother if necessary.

But the subject didn't come up again that evening.

On Thursday he came to her house after his therapy session, and after placating Bobby they went for a walk on the aqueduct. It had occurred to her that if her mother saw Brian in church with his parents, she might worry less about him. So she asked: "Do your parents ever go to church?"

"They went for my confirmation," he said. "But they haven't gone since then."

"Are they both Catholic?"

"They both were, but my mother doesn't believe in God anymore."

"You mean she's an atheist?"

"That's what she says."

"I never met an atheist."

"You can meet my mother if you want to." It didn't sound like an invitation.

"Where would I meet her? You said she never goes out."

"She doesn't. But I guess you could come to my house and meet her." It still didn't sound like an invitation.

"Do you want me to meet her?"

"No. I don't," he finally admitted.

"Are you afraid your mother won't like me?"

"I'm afraid she'll do a number on you."

"Well, I don't want to meet her, but at some point I should."

"I guess you should. But let's not spoil things now," he said, taking her hand.

On Friday she was surprised when Brian invited her to have dinner at his house. Since she had brought up the subject of meeting his parents, she couldn't say no, and since her parents were going out for dinner as usual, they didn't have any objections, so around six he came to get her in his car and drove her to his house, which was on Southlawn Avenue.

They found his mother in the living room, lying on the sofa. She raised her head and stared at Kerry as if she was a messenger bringing bad news.

"Mom, this is Kerry," Brian said.

"I'm glad to meet you," Kerry said politely.

"What's your last name?" his mother asked her.

"McGrath," she replied.

"How old are you?"

"I'm sixteen."

"Where do you live?"

"On Sheldon Place."

"What does your father do?"

"He's a teacher."

"Where does he teach?"

"In Yonkers."

The only question his mother didn't ask was: "What are you doing with my son?"

At that point his father appeared with a drink in one hand. His face was florid and his eyes were belligerent.

"Dad, this is Kerry," Brian said.

"I'm glad to meet you," Kerry said.

"So this is the girl you're tutoring," his father said, eyeing her in a way that made her feel naked.

"Yes," he said tensely.

"She's the reason you didn't go to baseball practice."

"No, she's not. The reason is I broke my arm."

"You still could have helped the pitchers."

"I tried. But I couldn't help them with my arm in a cast."

"You went one day, and then you quit," his father said, emphasizing the last word and making it sound like the worst thing a person could do.

"I couldn't help them," Brian insisted, raising his voice.

"You didn't want to help them. You wanted to see this girl."

"Jack," his mother said.

"I know what she's doing to you," his father said. "She's doing what your mother did to me."

"Jack, please."

His father stopped as if he recognized a danger sign, and he took a drink of whatever was in his glass—it looked like whisky.

"Come on," Brian said to Kerry. "We'll go and have a pizza."

"I thought you were going to have dinner with us," his mother said.

"I'm not going to stay and listen to that crap."

"He won't say any more about it. Will you, Jack."

His father growled and took another drink.

His mother got up from the sofa, saying: "Dinner's ready, so let's go and eat."

They went into the kitchen, where the table was set for four people. A bowl of potato salad, which looked as if it had come from a deli, was on the table.

"The fish are in the oven," his mother told Brian.

While his father poured himself another drink, Brian got a pan out of the oven. It was breaded fish filets, which looked like the kind you bought frozen. He set the pan down on the counter, with a trivet under it.

"I hope you like fish," his mother said to Kerry.

"Oh, yes," she said. "We have it often."

"I used to be a Catholic," his mother said, "so I'm in the habit of having fish on Friday."

Kerry didn't know what to say.

"Please sit down," his mother said.

She sat down, feeling uncomfortable and wishing they had gone for a pizza.

Brian brought two plates to the table with two pieces of fish on each of them. He set one plate in front of Kerry and the other in front of his mother.

"There's tartar sauce in the refrigerator," his mother told him.

When they had all sat down there was a silence as if they were going to say grace, but they started eating without a word.

His mother finally broke the silence, asking: "What does your mother do?"

"She's a lawyer. She works in the city."

"That sounds like more fun than staying at home all day."

"You don't have to stay at home all day," his father snorted.

"Yes. I do. In my condition I have no choice."

"There's nothing wrong with you. It's all in your head."

"That's easy to say," his mother said, "for people who have nothing in their heads."

"The fish is good," Kerry said, hoping to stop them.

"I caught it myself," his father said. "It's striped bass from the Hudson River."

Kerry knew it was cod, processed and frozen, but she didn't question him.

"We're not supposed to eat fish from the river," Brian said. "They're full of poison."

"I know," his father said. "I'm trying to kill you."

"Then you better not eat the fish yourself."

"My fish is different. It's from the supermarket. It's safe."

"Jack, please. You're not funny."

It didn't get better.

When they had finished eating, Brian said: "Kerry has to go home now."

"Why so early?" his mother asked.

"I promised her parents she'd be home by eight."

"Well, it's only seven-thirty."

"They don't want her to be late."

"All right," his mother said, sounding resigned.

His father poured himself another drink.

"Thanks for dinner," Kerry told them before she left, unable to bring herself to add: "I had a good time."

Neither of his parents said they hoped she would come again.

When they were on the aqueduct Brian asked: "So what do you think of my parents?"

"I don't like your father," she said honestly.

"I don't either."

"Why is he like that?"

"God knows. He's always been like that, at least as far back as I can remember."

"He made me feel it was my fault that you didn't go to baseball practice."

"I know he did. I'm sorry."

"And then he said I'm doing to you what your mother did to him. What did she do to him?"

"I told you. He quit playing baseball because of her."

"But that was years ago," she said, remembering. "And he still blames her?"

"Oh, yeah. It comes out every day in one form or another."

"Well, that must make her feel bad."

"It does. I mean, it makes her feel worse."

"What do you mean?"

They had stopped walking, and they faced each other.

"My mother's unhappy," Brian said with anguish in his eyes. "And I feel like it's my fault."

"Well, at times I feel like that about my mother."

"You do?" He gazed at her appreciatively.

"Yeah. But it's only a feeling, and it always goes away since I know it's not true."

"My feeling never goes away."

To make it go away, she kissed him, and he responded. For a long time they stood on the path kissing, and then she asked:

"Did that make your feeling go away?"

"Yeah," he said, smiling.

When she got home her parents were in the family room, reading.

"Did you have a good time?" her father said.

"Yeah," she said, thinking about what had happened on the aqueduct.

"What are his parents like?" her mother asked.

She shrugged. "They're parents."

"You mean typical parents?"

"Yeah. I guess."

Later, as she was going to bed her mother came into her room and asked: "Now, what were his parents really like?"

"They weren't typical."

"What do you mean?"

"Well, they don't act like they love each other."

"They don't even *act* like they do?"

"No. They act like they hate each other."

"How did they treat you?"

"His mother asked me a lot of questions, and his father made me feel it was my fault that Brian didn't go to baseball practice."

Her mother waited for her to continue.

"I know it wasn't my fault, so I can take it. But I don't know if I can take how Brian's parents make him feel."

"What do you mean?"

"His parents are unhappy," she explained, "and they make him feel like it's his fault."

Her mother nodded as if she had expected this. "So he has family problems."

"I guess he does. But I can help him."

With a sigh her mother sat down on the bed. "When I was a few years older than you, I got involved with a boy who was bright, attractive, and talented. He had everything going for him, except his parents. They hated each other, and they used him to hurt each other."

Kerry listened, knowing she was about to learn something important about her mother.

"They were tearing him apart. He didn't show it, but I knew what was happening to him. And because I loved him, I thought I could help him. But I failed. He got into drugs, and one night he took an overdose." Her mother grimaced as if the memory was still painful. "Of course I felt it was my fault. I felt that if only I'd said or done the right thing, I could have saved him. And I didn't get over it for a long time."

She understood. Her mother was afraid that she would get hurt the same way. But she didn't see how she could. "Don't worry. Brian wouldn't get into drugs."

"But if you think you can help him, you could still get hurt."

She still didn't see how she could. "How?"

"If you fail, you could feel like I did."

She didn't want to consider the risk. She believed that if you loved someone, you didn't think about yourself. "Well, don't worry. I can handle it."

"You have no idea what it's like."

"Yeah, I do. I've failed at a lot of things."

"Well, this is different."

"Maybe it is. But if I can help him—"

Her mother cut her off, saying: "I don't think you can."

Her mother had always encouraged her to do things she thought she couldn't, and now her mother was trying to discourage her. It confused her, but something deep inside of her asserted itself. "I think I can."

For a while her mother looked at her as if she was debating whether to tell her to stop seeing Brian, and then she said: "Okay. You can try. But don't get too involved with him. You know what I mean?"

"Yeah," she said, knowing what her mother meant and dismissing the possibility.

Her mother leaned over and kissed her goodnight.

While she lay in bed with the light out she thought about what had happened to her mother, and she concluded that if her mother had really loved that boy, she could have saved him.

EIGHT

NOW THAT BRIAN could drive again, they went off in his car on Saturday. As they left Henley she had a feeling of exhilaration. They were getting away from the confines of home, from the limits and roles imposed by their parents. She turned on the radio, found some music, rolled down the window, and reveled in the breeze.

They drove up Broadway through Dobbs Ferry and Irvington and then into Tarrytown, where they turned to get onto the Tappan Zee Bridge. The river below was peaceful and blue, reflecting the cloudless sky above.

As they crossed the bridge she sensed that Brian was getting away from his family problems.

They took the thruway to the Palisades Parkway and then went north toward Bear Mountain. The parkway rose and curved through the foothills, which were green with new leaves. It led them from one view to another.

"It's beautiful," she said, admiring the scenery.

"I'm glad you like it," he said happily.

"Do you come over here a lot?"

"Whenever I feel like getting away."

"By yourself?"

"Yeah. Most of the time. But sometimes with Mark."

"Is he your best friend?"

Brian considered. "I guess he is. He's the only guy I see outside of school. When you play three sports, you don't have much time for friends."

"If you played only one sport, which would you choose?"

"I don't know. I guess baseball."

"That's my father's favorite sport."

"If I wasn't a pitcher, I might not feel the same way. I mean, what I like is being on my own against the batter. It's up to me to stop him from getting on base."

"Do you miss playing it?"

"No. Not really. But if I hadn't met you, I might have."

"What if you hadn't met me?"

"I don't know what I would have done." For a moment it was as if they were going through a dark tunnel, and then they were out in the light again. "But I did meet you. And that changed everything."

They arrived at Bear Mountain, left the car, and got on the Appalachian Trail. They hiked for a while, heading north, and then they came to a high pass, where they stopped to look at a breathtaking view. Below was a valley, with a green meadow and a silver stream running through it. Beyond were the rounded peaks of mountains as far as you could see, rising in the distance and meeting the clouds.

"Wow," she said softly.

"It's really something, isn't it," he said.

They stood in silence, holding hands and sharing a feeling that she had never experienced before. It was like being shown the way to paradise.

Then some hikers came up behind them, breaking the spell.

"Come on," Brian said. He led her down the trail, away from the hikers. "It's better to come here during the week, when there aren't so many people around. We can do that this summer. I mean, if you want to."

"Yeah. I do."

They hiked a little farther, and then they turned back. It was after four, and he had to get her home by six or her parents would worry.

As they drove back across the bridge she sensed that he was returning to his family problems, and she put a hand on his shoulder to let him know she was still with him, no matter what side of the bridge he was on.

"Is there a party tonight?" he asked.

"Yeah. At Amanda's."

"Well, I'll come and get you at seven-thirty. Okay?"

"Okay." She wished he could have dinner at her house, but she didn't want to push things. And she didn't have to be home until twelve.

The boys were watching a Yankees game, and the girls were in the kitchen, talking about their plans for the summer. Amanda was hoping to get a job in a beauty parlor, Susan was going to a music camp, and Lisa was taking a computer course.

Kerry listened, not minding the fact that she had no plans for the summer.

"What are you going to do?" Amanda asked her.

"Oh, I'll do some babysitting, but that's all. I want to have time to spend with Brian."

"Does Brian have a job?"

"No. At least he hasn't mentioned having a job."

"Well, then see him as much as you can this summer. When football season comes around, you'll be glad you did. I know from experience."

"And then comes basketball season," Susan said.

"That's one good thing about Jerry," Lisa said. "He's not a jock."

"Speaking of jocks," Amanda said. "I think they've watched enough baseball."

"Yeah, let's get them away from the tube."

Six weeks passed without any major incident. She met with Brian on Monday, Tuesday, and Wednesday for tutoring, and also on Thursday after his therapy, which would end in the middle of June. Her grades in geometry improved, as did Bobby's fastball. They went to a party on Saturday, usually at Lisa's house since her parents usually went to a play, or a concert, or an opera in the city. Kerry went out for dinner on Friday with her family, and Brian never again suggested that she have dinner at his house. Occasionally, he stayed for dinner at her house during the week when her mother had to work late.

The last week of school, while they were walking along the aqueduct, Brian said: "I have some bad news. My father has a summer job for me."

"Where?" she asked.

"At the newspaper. And if I don't take it, I won't be able to live with him."

"Will you have to work every day?"

"Yeah. It's a full-time job."

"Then we won't be able to go across the river during the week."

"No. We won't."

They walked in silence, saddened by the loss of the time they had planned to spend together.

"He wanted me to go to baseball camp, but I refused. So the job was a compromise."

"Well, we can see each other at night," she said, putting her arm around him. "And we can go across the river on weekends."

"But I'll need to get away from them during the week."

"We can go to my place near the copper beech."

"I like that idea," he said, cheering up.

Brian started his job on Monday, and Kerry was alone at home since her father was in Yonkers, helping kids who had problems in school, and her brother was at baseball camp.

In the late afternoon she wandered down into the village and looked in the store windows for "Help Wanted" signs. She finally spotted one in the window of the health food store, and after staring at it for a while she mustered up the courage to go in and offer her services.

The woman, who had a pleasant face and braided blond hair, seemed to like her. But she also seemed to have some doubts. "How old are you?"

"I'm sixteen," Kerry said. If she had to prove it, she could show the woman her fake driver's permit.

"Have you ever worked in a store before?"

"No, but I can learn."

"Do you know how to cook?"

"I help my father cook dinner every night."

"Your father cooks dinner? What does your mother do?"

"She's a lawyer. She works in the city."

The woman nodded as if she understood. "Okay. You're hired. I'll need you at lunchtime when people come in and eat at the counter. The hours are from eleven to three. And the pay is five dollars an hour."

"That's sounds fine. When do I start?"

"Tomorrow if you can."

"I can," Kerry said, delighted. She had a job, her first real job, and she would be making a whole hundred dollars a week. She could buy a lot of things with that.

She left the store wanting to share her good fortune with someone. She looked at her watch. It was almost five, and Brian would be coming home soon.

She decided to go and meet him at the station.

But first she went to the ice cream store, which had just opened in time for summer, and she treated herself to a double chocolate cone.

Walking slowly, licking the ice cream, she headed down to the station.

She got a schedule and studied it. She figured that he would take the five-twenty, which arrived in Henley at five-fifty-five. So she went and waited on the platform. No one else was waiting there, though some wives were waiting in cars along with the taxi drivers.

She ate her cone, gazing at the red-brick factory building on the other side of the tracks. It belonged to the Anaconda Wire & Cable Company, but it had been abandoned years ago, so all it did now was block your view of the river. She had heard her parents talk about a plan to develop the waterfront that would give the village access to the river, but there was a major obstacle—the site was polluted, so until it was cleaned up, nothing could be built on it.

Kerry thought it would have been nice to walk down to the river and stroll along its bank, with a view of the Palisades, and she didn't understand why they didn't just tear down the building and clean up the site.

When the train came in she watched for Brian, hoping he was on it, though she was prepared to wait for the next train if necessary.

Then she saw him, marching along with the veteran commuters, with his tie loosened and his jacket slung over his shoulder, and his eyes downcast. She called to him, and when he saw her his face brightened.

She greeted him with a hug and a kiss, and holding hands, they headed up the hill.

"How was it?" she asked.

"Boring. I had nothing to do."

"Really?"

"Yeah. And when I asked if I could do something, they acted like I was bothering them. They told me to go and sit down, they'd talk to me later. But they never did. So I just sat there at a desk all day, doing nothing."

"If they don't need you, why did they hire you?"

"My father asked them to. I could tell it wasn't their idea."

"They're paying you, aren't they?"

"I guess they are."

"Then they'll find something for you to do."

"I hope so. If I have to sit around all day doing nothing, I'll go crazy."

"Don't worry. You won't."

"So what did you do?" he asked as they turned and headed up Spring Street.

"I sat around most of the day doing nothing, and then I decided to look for a job. And guess what," she said, squeezing his hand. "I found one."

"Where?"

"Over there." She pointed to the health food store. "I'm going to work for a nice lady, and I'm going to make a hundred a week."

"That's great," he said happily.

He went home with her, and he helped Bobby with his fastball. When her father took over he sat down next to her, and after her mother called to say she had to work late, he stayed for dinner. She helped her father make chicken cacciatore with linguine.

They sat at the picnic table and heaped their plates.

While they wolfed down the food Brian and Bobby talked about baseball. They wondered if the Mets could keep it up. They analyzed the pitching and batting statistics. From time to time her father joined the conversation, reminding them that even if the Mets made it to the World Series, they would still have to beat the Yankees.

Watching them and listening to them, Kerry was happy. Brian could have been a member of her family, and she wished for his sake that he had been her older brother so he wouldn't have parents who made him unhappy.

She arrived at the health food store about fifteen minutes early the next morning, and the woman, who said to call her Jeanne, started showing her what to do.

The food at lunchtime was served at a counter, which was actually an old wooden bar, a relic from the time when according to Jeanne the village had eighteen bars that served the men who worked at the Anaconda plant, three shifts a day. The menu was limited to soup, pita bread sandwiches, a salad of organic greens, yogurt, tofu, and various drinks, including herb teas and smoothies.

Jeanne made the soup every morning, starting at nine, and prepared the leaves for the salad, so all Kerry had to do was make the sandwiches and serve the customers.

About a dozen people came in for lunch at different times. They ranged from an elderly couple who had driven all the way from Tarrytown to buy organic dried fruits, to a Japanese housewife who walked over from a nearby apartment to buy seaweed. They were all nice to her, and they even tipped her. When she asked if she was supposed to keep the tips, Jeanne laughed and said of course. So she picked up a few extra dollars.

After lunchtime she cleaned up, and then she worked on the stock, which included all kinds of grains, nuts, fruits, vegetables, teas, oils, vitamins, and things she had never heard of. When she didn't know what something was she asked about it, and Jeanne told her. She felt that Jeanne would have made a good teacher.

She was packaging some dried figs from California, taking them from a crate and putting them into little plastic bags, when Jeanne pointed out that it was three o'clock.

"Okay," she said. She didn't want to leave since she liked what she was doing, and she didn't have anything else to do. "Can I just finish this?"

"Sure, if you want to."

"I mean, you don't have to pay me for the extra time."

Jeanne laughed. "Of course I'll pay you. As long as you're busy, you can stay."

"But I wasn't looking for more money."

"I know you weren't. But if you put in extra time, I'll pay you for it. That's only fair."

So she stayed another half hour and finished packaging the figs. Then she went home and waited until it was time to go and meet Brian.

On the following Monday, while they were making dinner, her mother called from Grand Central and said she would be on the six-twenty, so she would be home in time to eat with them.

Brian was still in the backyard when her mother got home.

"Can Brian stay for dinner?" she asked.

"Is he here?" her mother asked.

"Yeah. He's out in the backyard with Bobby."

"Well, I don't know. I don't often get home in time to eat with you."

"I know you don't. But you haven't ever talked with him and gotten to know him."

"Okay," her mother said, yielding. "He can stay for dinner."

Her mother didn't like eating at the picnic table, so they ate in the dining room, where it was no longer informal and relaxed. They acted differently, especially Brian, who no longer seemed like a member of the family. He seemed like a guest, unsure of his welcome.

"Where do you want to go to college?" her mother asked him.

"Harvard," he said without hesitation.

"That's a very good school. But why there?"

"It has a good psychology department, and if I go there, I can get into any graduate school."

"Do you want to be a psychologist?"

"Yeah. I want to help people who are mentally ill."

"Then maybe you want to be a psychiatrist."

"What's the difference?" Kerry asked.

"A psychologist talks with people," her mother explained. "A psychiatrist prescribes drugs."

"I don't want to be a psychiatrist," Brian said. "I don't think drugs help."

"Well, there's a lot of debate about that," her father said. "It's the old question of nature or nurture. The people who believe the problems are caused by nature favor drugs, whereas the people who believe the problems are caused by nurture favor therapy."

"In most cases," her mother said, "it's probably both."

"I think you get better results from therapy," Brian said.

"What do you base this opinion on?"

"Things I've read."

"Have you ever been in therapy?"

"No. I mean, except for my broken arm."

"That's physical therapy."

"I know. But it worked. If I'd just taken drugs, it wouldn't have helped."

Her mother didn't argue the point, but she still didn't look convinced.

When Brian had gone she overheard her parents talking in the kitchen.

"I'm troubled by the fact that he wants to be a psychologist," her mother said.

"I don't see why," her father said. "It's a good profession."

"Maybe it is. But the people I knew who became psychologists were fucked up."

"The one at my school isn't fucked up."

"People who want to help other people," her mother said, "are often driven by their own needs."

"I hope you don't include me in that group," her father said.

"I don't. You want to help other people because you have a lot to give."

"I think Brian has a lot to give. I mean, look what he's done for Kerry and Bobby."

"But he could be doing it to fulfill his own needs."

"He could be, but you don't know."

"I don't know," her mother admitted. "I just have a feeling."

"You're feeling could be wrong."

"But what if it's right?"

"Then she could get hurt. But I think we should give him the benefit of a doubt."

"Do you want to take that risk with your daughter?"

"I have faith in her. Whatever happens, I believe she'll do the right thing, and if she gets hurt, it'll make her stronger."

"Why do you think it'll make her stronger?"

"What happened to you made you stronger, didn't it?"

"It did. But even if Brian didn't have problems, I wouldn't want Kerry seeing him every day."

"Now, that's another issue."

"I think we should put a limit on the number of times per week she sees him."

"What do you suggest?"

"Twice a week."

"Oh, I don't know. That's really strict."

"It's as often as we saw each other when we were dating."

"But you were going to law school, and that was a limit we imposed on ourselves."

"Then what do you suggest?"

"Three times a week."

"All right. I'll tell her."

"I'll tell her. You don't have to be the bad guy."

"Yeah. I do. I'm married to a good guy."

She was getting ready for bed when her mother came into her room. She knew what her mother was going to say, and she was ready to argue.

"Your father and I were talking," her mother said, "and we agreed that you're seeing too much of Brian."

"I only see him for a few hours."

"But you see him every day."

"What's wrong with that?"

"There's nothing wrong with it," her mother said. "It's just too much."

"Well, you see Dad every day. Is that too much?"

"Your father and I are married."

Kerry had no argument there since she wasn't about to say that she and Brian were going to get married. She hadn't thought that far ahead.

"I know you want to help him," her mother continued, "and maybe you can. But you won't be able to help him if you get too involved with him. And if you see him every day, you *will* get too involved with him."

"But we're not alone. We're here with Dad and Bobby."

"You still see him every day. And it's too much." Her mother paused. "From now on, you can see him only three times a week."

"That's not enough," she protested.

"It's more than your father and I saw each other when we were dating."

"I don't care. It's not enough."

"I'm not going to argue with you. That's the limit. Trust us," her mother added, "we know what's best for you."

The next day, while she waited for Brian at the station, she wondered how she was going to tell him. She knew he was going to be upset, but there was nothing she could do about it. She had tried to get her father to extend the limit, but he had agreed with her mother. So now she had to tell Brian she could see him only three times a week.

When the train arrived she greeted him as usual, and they started walking up the hill, holding hands. There were people around them, so she couldn't tell him yet. Instead, she asked: "How was your day?"

"It was better," he said. "At least they found something for me to do. How was your day?"

"Oh, it was all right."

He looked at her. "What's wrong?"

"My mother set another limit. From now on, I can see you only three times a week."

He stopped. "Why?"

"She thinks I'm getting too involved with you."

"Does that mean you can't see me tonight?"

"Well, tonight would be the second time this week, and if we go to Lisa's on Saturday, that would be the third time. So if I see you tonight, then I couldn't see you until Saturday."

"Does meeting me at the station count?"

"I guess it does. But not this time since I had to tell you about the limit."

"Then maybe we should meet on Wednesday or Thursday."

"Maybe we should. How about Thursday?"

"Why not Wednesday?"

"That's tomorrow, and I saw you today."

"Okay," he said dejectedly.

They continued walking up the hill.

"Do you want to see me?" he asked after a long silence.

"Yeah," she said. "I want to see you every day, but my parents won't let me."

They walked in silence up Main Street to Five Corners, where they crossed Broadway and got onto the aqueduct.

When they stopped at her gate he asked: "Do you love me?"

"Yes." She could see from the look in his eyes that he didn't believe it, so she tried to prove it by kissing him, but she realized that kissing him wasn't enough. She made a quick decision and said: "I'll meet you after dinner tonight."

"What'll you tell your parents?"

"I'll tell them I'm going to Amanda's house."

"Where will you meet me?"

"On the aqueduct."

"Where on the aqueduct?"

"Below your house."

"What time?"

"At eight."

"Okay. I'll be there waiting for you."

"I'll see you then," she said, making a promise.

She kissed him goodbye, and she lingered there to watch him go, already justifying the lie she would tell her parents.

When she went into the kitchen Bobby asked: "Where's Brian?"

"He isn't coming today," she said, reaching for a cookie with an unsteady hand.

"Why isn't he?"

"Because Mom doesn't want me to see him every day."

"Well, that sucks. I was making progress."

"I know you were." She wished she had thought of her brother's pitching as an argument, though it probably wouldn't have carried much weight.

"Is he coming tomorrow?"

"No, not until Thursday."

"That really sucks. I'll have to practice my fastball with Dad."

While he was doing that she called Amanda and told her what had happened.

"My mother set a limit," Amanda said, "when I started dating Kevin. But she enforced it less and less. So don't worry. Your mother will too."

"But what did you do in the meantime?"

"I got around it."

"That's what I'm going to do," she said, reinforced by the fact that her friend had done the same thing. "I told Brian I'd meet him after dinner tonight."

"And you don't want your parents to know?"

"That's right. If I tell them I'm at your house, will you cover for me?"

"Of course I will. Do you think they'll check on you?"

"No. They trust me. But in case they call looking for me, will you tell them I just left?"

"I'll do better than that. I'll have my sister tell them we went to the village. So they'll have no way of contacting you."

She thanked Amanda, and then she started making dinner, hoping that her mother would call to say she had to work late. It would be harder to deceive her mother, though it would be harder to lie to her father. She had never lied to him before, and she felt bad just thinking about it. But she felt worse thinking how Brian would feel if she didn't show up. Besides, she had made a promise, and considering her alternatives, she had no doubt that breaking a promise was a greater sin than telling a lie, especially since she would only be lying to get around the unfair limit that her parents had imposed on her.

When her mother called to say that she had to work late, Kerry knew she had a better chance of getting away with it. But she had to work herself up to lying to her father.

While they were cleaning up after dinner she told him: "I'm going to Amanda's."

"Would you like a ride there?"

"No, thanks. I can walk."

"Well, don't go on the aqueduct."

"I won't," she said, knowing she would break this promise.

As she was leaving, her father said: "Have a good time."

She felt awful, knowing he trusted her completely. But she also knew that Brian was waiting for her, counting on her. And she couldn't let him down.

Hurrying along the aqueduct, she vividly remembered her father's warnings about walking here alone at night, and she imagined a rapist lurking behind every tree. So she was relieved when she spotted Brian ahead of her.

"I thought you wouldn't come," he said.

"I told you I would."

"Well, I was afraid your parents would stop you."

"My mother wasn't home yet, so it was easier to get away." She didn't tell him what it had cost her to lie to her father since that would make him feel bad.

"Where do you want to go?" he asked.

"To the copper beech," she said, taking his hand.

They followed the path through Dobbs Ferry and across the campus of Mercy College, and they arrived at the copper beech in time for the sunset.

Sitting on the hillside, they gazed out at the wide river, which turned from pink to blue to gray as the light gradually faded from the sky. Then they lay back, and in the privacy of the night they started kissing.

When she felt him wanting more of her she unzipped her jeans and peeled them off, and there on the grass she proved she loved him.

NINE

WHEN SHE GOT home she heard her parents in the family room, and though she would have preferred to avoid them, she decided not to go upstairs without reporting to them. If she did, they might suspect something.

"Hi," she said, showing herself in the doorway. She was afraid that her mother could tell just by looking at her that she had made love with Brian.

"Hi," her mother said languidly. "How was Amanda?"

"Oh, she was fine."

"You should ask her to cut your hair again. It's getting long."

"I guess it is."

"Does Amanda have a boyfriend?"

"Yeah. His name is Kevin."

"Does she see him every day?"

"No. But she could if she wanted to."

"Then I give her credit for not getting too involved with him."

She let this pass since it wouldn't have helped to point out that Amanda and Kevin had been making love since last year. She just said: "I'm going to bed."

"Goodnight," her father said. "We love you."

She paused on the stairs to listen, but they weren't talking about her. They were talking about her mother's work. They evidently had no idea what she had done.

Sitting on the toilet, she noticed the dark stain in her panties, and after undressing she washed them out in the bathroom sink. It had been the only evidence, and now that she had removed it she didn't see how they could catch her.

Unless she got pregnant. She was stunned by the thought, and frantically she counted the days back to the end of her last period. It was seven days, or maybe eight. And she remembered from sex education that you were fertile between the twelfth and the sixteenth day.

But then she couldn't remember if you counted from the end of your period or from the beginning. If it was the beginning, then she was in the twelfth or thirteenth day of her cycle, and she was in the danger zone. She lay awake, worrying. If she was pregnant, she couldn't have an abortion. That was against her religion, and it was a major issue of her church. In fact, it was included in the petitions every Sunday. And the thought of being prayed for as one of those people who had killed a baby made her want to die.

But if she had a baby, it would ruin Brian's life, and it would greatly embarrass her parents, to say the least. A girl in the class ahead of her got pregnant last fall, and the whole village talked about it. The family finally moved away.

Tossing and turning, she worked herself into a sweat. She prayed that she wasn't pregnant, and she promised not to do it again.

The next day, as they walked up from the train station, she told Brian about her worry. "The thing is, I can't remember if you count from the beginning or the end of your period."

"You count from the beginning," he said.

"So I'm in the twelfth or thirteenth day of my cycle."

"Don't worry. You're not pregnant."

"But what if I am?"

"Then we'll get married."

"We're not old enough to get married without the consent of our parents. I mean, not in the state of New York."

"Then we'll go to another state."

"But if we get married and have a baby, what will happen to your dream of going to Harvard and being a psychologist?"

"I'll still achieve it. I'll just have to work a little harder."

She appreciated his support, though she wondered if he was being realistic. "Well, if I'm not pregnant, I won't want to take a chance again."

"We won't," he said as if he would take care of it.

They turned onto Main, and when they arrived at the drugstore he said: "Wait. I won't be long."

Instead of waiting in front of the drugstore, she wandered down to the store where she had bought the pink sweater, and she looked idly at things in the window. It seemed like ages ago that she had bought that sweater.

"We're all set," he said, rejoining her.

She assumed he had bought condoms, which were being recommended and even advertised for safe sex. She didn't care what else they were good for as long as they stopped her from getting pregnant, though using them would add another sin to her growing list.

They parted on the aqueduct, and she watched him go, feeling that whether or not his life was in her body, it was in her hands.

On Thursday she was allowed to see him, so she brought him home from the station and watched him help Bobby with his pitching. Since her mother had to work late, he stayed for dinner, and things were almost the way they had been.

On Friday she met him at the station, but she didn't bring him home since she was going out for dinner with her family, so they didn't have a chance to be together.

On Saturday, which was the Fourth of July, she had dinner with her family and then went with her friends to the campus of Mercy College, where you could see the fireworks in Dobbs Ferry and even in the city. She had arranged to meet Brian there, and after they had watched the fireworks for a while they walked over to the aqueduct and went to their place near the copper beech. As she unzipped her jeans she remembered her promise not to do it again, but by now she was in so deep that one more sin didn't matter.

On Sunday at mass she bowed her head during the penitential

rite and asked God to forgive her sins, which in addition to the usual sins included lying to her father, breaking her promise not to go on the aqueduct at night, making love with Brian, breaking her promise not to do it again, and using condoms.

Now she was going to hell, yet only a week ago she still had a chance of going to heaven. But she couldn't confess to Father Joseph since he would know who she was, and he would be disappointed in her. All she could do was join in the paryer: "Lord, have mercy. Christ, have mercy. Lord, have mercy."

The worst thing was leaving the church and walking by Our Lady of the River, who looked at her as if she was deeply worried about her. She would have walked the other way to avoid Our Lady, but she had to stay with her family

The next morning, while she was having breakfast, the phone rang. She was alone in the house since her brother had left for baseball camp and her father had left for Yonkers.

It was Brian, who said: "I'll be on the nine-twenty train. Can you meet me at the station?"

"Yeah. What happened?"

"I'll tell you later. I have to catch the train."

"Okay," she said, wondering if he had quit his job. If he had, it would make things worse with his father. And it would be all her fault.

By the time she spotted him getting off the train she was ready to talk him into going back.

"I quit my job," he said happily.

"Why?" she asked.

"It was boring."

"I thought it was getting better."

"Naw. They didn't give me enough to do. They didn't need me. They only hired me because of my father."

"Well, I think you should go back."

"You're kidding."

"I'm not."

"But now we can see each other every day, and you don't have to lie to your parents."

"I've gotten used to lying to them. I'm more concerned about your father. Quitting your job will make things worse."

"Fuck him," Brian said. "I want to be free during the day. I want to go across the river and hike on the Appalachian Trail, just liked we planned. Don't you?"

"I do, but—"

"Then come with me, and stop talking about my father."

"Okay," she said, going with him.

On their way up the hill she had to stop at the health food store and tell Jeanne she would no longer be able to work there. She felt bad about doing this since Jeanne had been so nice to her, but she owed it to Brian to quit her job too.

They stopped at her house, where she made peanut butter and jelly sandwiches to take with them, and then they took the path to his house.

Following him into the kitchen, she was struck by the fact that there were no coffee mugs in the sink, no papers on the table, and no notes on the refrigerator. It was as if no one lived there. "Is your mother home?"

"She's always home."

"What does she do all day?"

"Nothing. Wait here. I'll be right back."

She stayed in the kitchen while he went upstairs.

"Who is it?" his mother called out, sounding frightened.

"It's me," he said.

"What are you doing home?"

"I quit my job."

"You did? Why?"

"They didn't give me enough to do."

"Your father will be very upset."

Brian said nothing.

She heard him walking around upstairs and then starting back down.

"Where are you going?" his mother asked.

"Across the river."

"I hope you're not running away."

"I'm not. I'll be back tonight."

There was a cry, followed by another, and then a long heart-rending wail. It made her feel awful, and she could only imagine how it made Brian feel.

He came into the kitchen carrying a backpack, looking sick.

"Does she do that often?"

"Yeah, all the time."

"So what's wrong with her?"

"God knows," he said despondently.

"Let's get out of here," she said, sensing how much he wanted to escape.

As they left the village she stopped worrying about his father and his mother. She and Brian had the whole day to spend together, and they would have the next day, and the day after that for the rest of the summer.

They crossed the bridge and took the parkway up to Bear Mountain. They got on the trail, glad to find that there were almost no people around since it was a week day. They stopped at the high pass, and as they stood there admiring the view, she noticed something.

"Look," she said, pointing.

"What?" he asked, searching.

"That patch of blue. It looks like a lake."

"Oh, yeah. I never noticed that before."

"Do you think we could find it?'

"I think we could. Let's try."

She had the feeling that if they could only find that lake, they would be in paradise.

They followed the trail as long as it went in the right direction, and then they left it, striking off into the woods. She realized that they could get lost, but she didn't worry. In fact, she wished that for Brian's sake they would get lost and never find their way back again.

"It should be around here somewhere," he said after a while.

"The thing is, it could be here, or it could be there, or over there, and we wouldn't see it."

"If I were the lake, where would I be?" she said, closing her eyes. She concentrated, drawing on her instincts, and she made a guess. "I think it's over there."

They pushed through the woods and climbed a hill, and there it was.

"You were right," he said, elated.

"I was lucky," she admitted.

The lake was small and perfectly round, with a rim of beach. Its surface was like a mirror, reflecting the trees on the far shore, the sky, the clouds, and finally the mountains.

There was no sign of people around it, no sign that anyone else had discovered it.

"This is it," he said, meaning everything.

"And it's ours," she said, claiming it for them.

They found a comfortable spot on the beach and spread the blanket he had packed.

Then he said: "Let's go swimming."

They hadn't brought swimsuits, but there was no one around, and no one was going to come upon them. Still, she was a little shy since he hadn't seen her naked yet. And she waited for him to go first. Then seeing how much he was enjoying it, she shed her clothes.

She scampered into the water and immediately took to swimming in the nude. It was as if after being in a cage all her life, she had been returned to her natural habitat and set free. She laughed and frisked around in the water, she jumped for joy.

When they got out they sprawled on the blanket and let the sun dry them. They gazed at each other, admired each other, touched each other, and loved each other.

"I wish we could stay here forever," he said as they lay beside each other.

"I do too." If she had been a cat, she would have been purring.

"I never imagined it was possible to be so happy."

"Well, it *is* possible." Whatever she had done for him, he had done the very same thing for her. By accepting her love he had made her believe she had something to offer, he had given her a feeling of worth.

She was sitting on the back steps, watching her father and Bobby play catch, when her mother got home. She could tell that something good had happened.

"We got the ruling," her mother said triumphantly.

"You did?" her father said. "That's great."

"What's a ruling?" Bobby asked.

"A decision by the court," his father explained.

She looked at her mother. "Does that mean you've won?"

"Well, not quite. But we have the upper hand now. And if we don't blow it, we'll win."

"I think we should celebrate," her father said.

"Why don't you take Mom out to dinner," Kerry suggested.

"You read my mind."

"But you've already made dinner, haven't you?" her mother said.

"We've only made the sauce. We haven't started to cook the pasta."

"Then maybe we should all go out."

"I don't feel like going out," Kerry said.

"I don't either," Bobby said. "Kerry and I can have pasta."

"So change into something comfortable," her father said, "and I'll make a reservation."

By the time they left, she and Bobby had finished eating, and as soon as she had cleaned up she called Brian.

He answered after only one ring.

"It's me," she said.

"I thought it was you."

"You did? Really?"

"I had a feeling."

"I called to tell you what a great time I had today."

"I had a great time too," he said softly.

"Is your father home yet?"

"No. Net yet. He usually doesn't get home until late."

"You mean he has to work late?"

"No. He goes out drinking after work with the other reporters."

"So what'll he do when he gets home?"

"He'll yell at me for quitting my job. But I won't let him bother me. I'll think about what we did today, and what we're going to do tomorrow."

"Okay. I love you."

"I love you too."

She was in bed, with her light turned off, when her parents got home. And she lay still, pretending to be asleep, when her mother looked into her room.

She heard their door close, and then she heard the sounds of their making love. No longer mysterious, the sounds reassured her, not only confirming the physical bond between her parents but also validating the bond between her and Brian.

The next morning, while she was having breakfast, Brian came to the back door. It was after nine, so no one else was there, but she was surprised to see him since she had been planning to meet him at his house an hour later.

"What's wrong?" she asked, letting him in.

"My father took the keys to my car."

"He did? Oh, no."

"And he won't give them back to me unless I go back to that fucking job."

"Well, maybe you should."

"If I do, then we won't be able to go across the river during the week. We won't be able to go back to our lake."

"But if you don't go back to your job, you won't have a car."

"I can get another car."

"You can? How?"

"I can buy one."

"Do you have enough money?"

"Yeah. I think so. Do you have the local paper?"

She found the *Herald Statesman*, which her father got every Sunday along with the *Times*.

Brian spread the paper on the table and looked at the ads. He identified several prospects, but when he called them he found that the people couldn't show him their cars until after work, so he could only make appointments with them.

They had the whole day ahead of them and the whole house to themselves, at least until five when her brother got home, so she and Brian could do what they wanted without any risk of being caught.

"Come on," she said, taking his hand. "I'll show you my room."

They spent the next several hours in her bed. He didn't have a condom, but she was no longer worried about getting pregnant. She could even imagine how their problems would be solved by her having a baby.

Around five he got Mark to drive him around and look at cars, and she went with him since she was allowed to see him that night.

The first car was in Yonkers. It was a 1973 Ford, owned by a man who greeted them with a can of Bud in his hand. There were dents in the fenders and rust on the doors, and when they drove it there was a sound of potential trouble, which Mark said was the transmission.

"I wouldn't buy it," Mark said. "If you do, you'll have to put three hundred dollars into it."

So they moved on, going to another part of Yonkers.

After looking at five cars, all of which Mark advised him not to buy, Brian was running out of patience.

"For what I'm paying," he told Mark, "I'm not going to find a perfect car. So just tell me which one will give me the least amount of trouble."

"Well, it's hard to say." Mark explained how with one of the cars he might have to replace the transmission, and with another he might have to overhaul the engine. "They're all big jobs, and they'll cost you more than you paid for the car."

"So what should I do?"

"Keep looking."

The next was a 1975 Chevy, which had only twenty thousand miles on it. Mark suspected that the odometer had gone around and started over, but the owner said that the car had belonged to his invalid mother, who had hardly ever used it.

They drove the car around the block, and it sounded all right. Mark raised the hood and looked at the engine, then crawled under the car with his flashlight.

"Well?" Brian asked.

"I wouldn't buy it."

"Why not?"

"You'd have to replace the radiator."

"There's nothing wrong with the radiator," the owner said.

"Yeah, there is. It's rusted."

"So what's a little rust? It's a radiator, for godsake. It's exposed to water."

"It'll have to be replaced, and that'll cost two hundred dollars."

"Two hundred dollars? You're full of shit."

"Well, I wouldn't buy it," Mark said, "unless he takes two hundred dollars off his price."

The man finally agreed to take two hundred off, so Brian bought the car. They drove it to Mark's house, where there was room in the driveway for another car. In fact, there was room for several other cars since most of the yard had been paved over.

"What about the radiator?" Brian asked when they had parked the car.

"You should have it checked," Mark said.

"Can I use the car in the meantime?"

"Yeah. But I wouldn't take it on a trip."

The next morning, after buying liability insurance from an agent in Dobbs Ferry, they went to Yonkers on the train to register the car, which took all morning. Then they went to Yonkers in the car to have the radiator checked by a guy that Mark had recommended.

The guy, whose name was Vinnie, examined the radiator and said he could fix it.

"How much would it cost?" Brian asked.

"Since you're a friend of Mark's, a hundred dollars."

"That's fine. How long will it take?"

"I can't do it now, but if you bring it in next Tuesday, I can do it then."

"You can't do it any sooner?"

"No. There're a lot of people ahead of you."

"Okay. I'll bring it in on Tuesday."

They left the car at Mark's house, and they spent a blissful hour in her bed, setting her alarm to make sure that Bobby didn't catch them there asleep.

The next morning, as soon as her father had left the house, she called Brian.

"What do you want to do today?" she asked him.

"I want to go across the river."

"Mark said not to take the car on a trip."

"Well, I think he meant like a trip to Boston. We're only going fifty miles."

"What if something happens?"

"If the car overheats, we just have to wait until it cools down."

"Okay," she said since she knew nothing about cars.

They were driving north on the parkway when something blew and a cloud rose from under the hood.

"Oh, shit," Brian said. He pulled over to the side of the road and stopped the car.

"What happened?" she asked.

"I think we blew a hose."

They got out, and Brian raised the hood.

The engine was smoking, and it smelled like when she had left a kettle on the stove and the water had all boiled away.

"It wasn't a hose," Brian said grimly. "It must have been the radiator."

"Do we just have to wait until it cools down?"

"I don't know. I hope so."

They waited for about a half hour, and then he tried starting the car. But it wouldn't start.

After waiting longer and trying again he finally said: "It won't start."

"So what are we going to do?"

"We're going to hitch a ride to the nearest gas station."

That was easier said than done. At least a hundred cars zoomed by before anyone stopped for them. The driver of the car that finally did stop, a guy with shades and slicked-back hair, took a look under the hood and said: "Your engine's shot."

"Can it be fixed?"

"I wouldn't bother."

Kerry put a hand on Brian's shoulder, knowing how he felt.

The guy drove them to a gas station, where Brian arranged to have the car towed. Luckily, he had money on him, what he had been going to pay Vinnie.

Then they had to figure out how to get home.

Mark was at work, so he couldn't help them now. So she called the beauty shop, and Amanda came and rescued them.

The next morning, while she was having breakfast, Brian came to her house and gave her the bad news about the car. After looking at it, Mark had advised him to junk it.

"I'm sorry," she told him, feeling bad for him.

"It's my fault," he said. "I should have listened to Mark and Vinnie. But I wanted to go across the river. I wanted to go back to our lake."

"I know. I did too."

"And now we don't have a way to get there."

"Don't worry. We'll find a way."

He thought for a moment. "The only way is to get my car keys from my father."

"How would you do that?"

"He must have put them somewhere."

"He could have them with him."

"I don't think so. I think they're somewhere in the house."

"Well, if you're going to look for them, I'll help you."

They walked on the aqueduct to his house and went in the back door. Though it was his house, she felt like they were burglars.

"Is your mother upstairs?"

"No. My father took her to the doctor."

"What if they come back and find us here?"

"They won't be back for a while," he assured her.

They looked in the kitchen, and then they went into the study, where his father sometimes worked at home. They searched through all the drawers of the desk and on all the bookshelves, but they didn't find the keys.

They went upstairs and into his parents' bedroom. They were going through his father's socks in the top drawer of a bureau when they heard a sound in the kitchen.

"They can't be back already," Brian said.

But they were, and they started coming upstairs, talking.

"Your doctor's full of shit," his father said.

"He knows what he's doing," his mother said.

Kerry and Brian were leaving the bedroom when his parents reached the top of the stairs.

"What the hell are you doing here?" his father asked angrily.

"I'm looking for my car keys," Brian said.

"Well, you're not going to find them. I have them with me. And I'm not going to give them back to you."

"It's my car."

"I paid for it."

"I'll buy it from you."

"It's not for sale."

"Jack, please. I want to lie down."

They stopped arguing only long enough for his mother to shuffle into the bedroom.

"Come on," Brian said. "Let's get out of here."

"You're not going anywhere," his father said, blocking the way, "until you've explained what you were doing here."

"I told you. I was looking for my car keys."

"You don't need a girl to do that."

"She offered to help me."

"Yeah. Sure." His father looked at her as if she was a piece of shit. "I don't like what you're doing to my son."

"I'm not doing anything to him," she said, trying not to be afraid of his father.

"You're the reason he quit his job."

"She's not the reason," Brian said, defending her.

"And you're the reason he didn't go to baseball camp."

"She's not," Brian said, raising his voice.

"If you hadn't fallen for this girl, you would have gone to baseball camp."

"I wouldn't have."

"You would have. You loved baseball."

"I liked it," Brian said. "But I never loved it the way you do."

"You did love it. But now you love this girl more."

"I do love her more. She's a human being. Baseball is only a game."

"I know what she's doing to you. She's doing what your mother did to me."

"Stop it," his mother screamed from the bedroom.

His father stopped, but only for a moment. "If you don't wake up, you're going to regret it for the rest of your life."

"Get out of my way," Brian said menacingly.

For a moment it looked as if they were going to tangle with each other, but then his father stepped aside and let them pass.

Outside, they got on the aqueduct and started walking.

"I'm sorry," he said after a while.

"It's not your fault."

"He makes me feel like it *is* my fault."

"But what did you ever do to him?"

"I was born," Brian said hopelessly. "My father quit playing baseball because of me."

"It was their decision to have a baby, not yours."

"It wasn't a decision. It was an accident."

"How do you know?"

"He told me."

Imagining how it had made him feel, she hated his father. And she put her arm around his waist to let him know that whether or not his parents had wanted him, she did.

TEN

THEY WANTED TO buy another car, but they no longer had enough money, so on Monday they started looking for work.

They took a bus to Central Avenue, and after going to several fast-food restaurants they found jobs at a McDonald's. They figured that after working three weeks they would have enough money to buy an old car. Of course by then there wouldn't be much left of the summer, but at least they would have a few weeks of freedom before football practice started.

Along with the money, the good things about the job were that they would have the same shift, so during the day they would be together, and their hours were from seven to three, so they would be free for the remainder of the afternoon. The only bad thing would be getting up at five-thirty and taking the bus to Central Avenue.

They were going to start training on Tuesday, so Kerry had to tell her parents about the job. But she couldn't reveal the fact that she would be with Brian since there was still a limit on how many times a week she could see him.

Later that evening, after waiting for an opportune moment, she found her parents in the family room, reading.

"I have a new job," she announced proudly.

"You do?" her mother said, looking up. "Where?"

"At McDonald's, on Central Avenue."

Her mother made a face. "McDonald's?"

"Yeah. It's a good job."

"What would you be doing?"

"Taking orders."

"Are you old enough to work there?"

"Yeah." She had shown them her fake driver's permit.

"How would you get there?" her father asked.

"I can take the bus."

"Will anyone else you know be working there?" her mother asked.

"No. My friends have other jobs."

"I thought you liked your job at the health food store."

"I did. But I wasn't making enough money."

"Why do you need money?"

"To buy clothes."

"If you need clothes, we'll buy them. We don't expect you to be financially independent."

"Well, I don't like having to ask for money."

"All right," her mother said. "It could be a good experience for you."

At five-thirty the next morning she was jolted by her alarm, and in order to raise herself out of bed she reminded herself that they had a goal, and also that she would only have to do this for three weeks.

Munching on a doughnut, she went out the front door and walked to Broadway, where Brian was waiting at the bus stop. By the time her mother walked to the station they would be gone, so there was no risk of her seeing them together.

When they arrived at McDonald's a skinny man with glasses explained the job to them. The people who ran the business had thought of everything, so you didn't have to think for yourself. You only had to follow procedures. She could see right away that she wasn't going to learn as much here as she had at the health food store, but that didn't matter.

During the peak hours when they were busy serving customers the time passed quickly, and in between when they weren't so busy she could talk with Brian. So it wasn't bad, though when three o'clock came she didn't feel like staying any longer.

When they got back to Henley they went to her house.

"Would you like a Coke?" she asked as they stood in the kitchen.

"I'd like some water," he said. "I'm thirsty."

She got a glass, and after running the water a while she filled it for him.

"Have some," he told her. "You must be thirsty too."

"I am." She drank from the glass and then gave it to him. Wiping her mouth, she sniffed the back of her hand. "Oh, shit. I smell like a Big Mac."

He sniffed his arm. "I do too."

"I need to take a shower."

"Okay," he said as if he would wait for her.

She had a sudden, daring idea. "We could take a shower together."

"We only have an hour before your brother gets home."

"That's enough time. Come on," she said, taking his hand.

She led him upstairs.

They went into the bathroom that she shared with her brother. She closed the door, and they shed their clothes and stood naked, facing each other.

He reached out and touched her.

She touched him.

They made love, standing, and then they got into the shower.

Letting the water flow over her head, with her eyes closed, she felt as if her sins were being washed away.

It became a routine. They would leave work promptly at three and get back to Henley around three-thirty and go to her house and take a shower.

Unless it was a day when Kerry was allowed to see him, Brian would be gone by the time her brother or her father came home. They probably could have trusted Bobby to keep their secret, but they didn't want to take any chances.

One afternoon, during their second week at McDonald's, they were in the shower when someone pounded on the door.

Her heart stopped.

"Are you almost done?" her brother asked.

"No. I'm not. If you can't hold it, use the other bathroom."

"Mom doesn't like me using their bathroom."

"Well, that's because you pee on the floor. Just try to be careful."

She turned off the shower, and while Brian started to dry himself she went out into the hall with a towel wrapped around her, looking for Bobby.

A few minutes later she saw her brother coming out of the other bathroom.

"Why are you taking a shower now?" he asked her.

"I smelled like a Big Mac," she said.

"I like that smell."

"Well, I don't like it after working at McDonald's all day. And don't ever do that again."

"Do what?" Her brother looked at her innocently.

"Pound on the door when I'm in the shower. You scared the shit out of me."

"Did you think I was a psycho killer?"

"Yeah. So don't ever do it again."

"Well, a psycho killer wouldn't have knocked. He would have just gone in and killed you."

"You didn't knock, you pounded on the door."

"If I hadn't, you wouldn't have heard me."

She wondered what he meant. She tried to remember if they had been making a lot of noise. She didn't think so, but if Bobby had caught them she would have to ask him not to tell.

She waited for her brother to go downstairs, and then she went back into the bathroom.

"Were we making a lot of noise?" she asked Brian, who was dressed.

"No. We weren't."

"Then he didn't catch us."

"He still might."

"Not if we're careful. I'll get dressed and occupy him in the kitchen, and you can go out the front door."

"Okay," he said. "I guess we better not do this again."

"We better not. But after next week we'll have a car, and then we can go to our lake."

He brightened at the thought. "Yeah."

During their third week at McDonald's they looked for a car, again with Mark's help. After driving to Yonkers, New Rochelle, and Mt. Vernon they found a 1979 Chevy that only needed work on the brakes. And this time they waited until Vinnie fixed it.

By now it was August, and there wasn't much left of the summer since football practice started in two weeks. So the morning they picked up the car at Vinnie's they packed a lunch and drove across the river.

When they arrived at Bear Mountain they noticed that there were more people around, probably because more people took vacations in August. But it still wasn't as bad as a weekend, and they were going to a place that no one knew about.

They had only been there once, and that had been a month ago, so they had to stop at the high pass and relocate the lake.

"There it is," she said, pointing.

"Yeah," he said happily.

From there it still looked like paradise.

They hurried down the trail. They found the place where they had struck off into the woods, and they followed their instincts the rest of the way. But when they came over the hill they were horrified by what they saw.

Across the water, on the very spot where they had spread their blanket, two naked people were engaged in a sexual act, the woman on her hands and knees and the man mounted on top of her, brutally pumping. Whatever they were feeling, it sounded like pain, and she was reminded of a painting she had seen in a museum that depicted couples in many positions suffering the torments of hell.

Around the couple was strewn the garbage from their lunch.

She put her arm around Brian, knowing they would never come here again and wanting to comfort him in their loss.

"Come on," he said softly.

They walked back to the trail in silence.

Then they stopped. Without the lake as a destination they had nowhere to go.

Brian stood there, staring gloomily into the woods.

"We'll find another lake," she told him, trying to raise his spirits.

"Where?" he asked doubtfully.

"I don't know. But somewhere we'll find one."

"Do you promise to go wherever it is?"

"Yes. I promise."

They were sitting at the picnic table, having dinner.

"I think they can still win the pennant," Bobby said as he took some more potato salad.

"Not if they play like they did last night," his father said. "They left too many men on base."

"They just weren't hitting."

"They should have bunted. If you have a man on first and no outs, you should move him to second. But Johnson tells them to hit away."

"Well, it works when they're hitting."

"It works when they're lucky."

"The worst thing about him," Brian said, "is he doesn't know when to replace pitchers."

"He doesn't," her father agreed. "He either takes them out too soon or leaves them in too long. And last night he should have left Fernandez in."

"Yeah. He should have."

After taking another piece of chicken her father asked: "When does football practice start?"

"On Monday," Brian said.

"Are we going to have a good team?"

"We should. We didn't lose too many people."

"We're going to beat Dobbs Ferry this year," Bobby said as if it was a sure thing.

"Oh, I don't know," Brian said. "They've been undefeated for three years."

"Then it's time they got defeated," her father said.

"Yeah. It is," Bobby said.

"We're going to try," Brian said.

"How's your arm?" her father asked.

"It seems okay. It hasn't bothered me throwing a baseball."

"Well, maybe you should start throwing a football."

"No, not yet," Bobby said. "I still haven't perfected my curve."

His father laughed. "You can do that next year."

After dinner she and Brian went for a walk on the aqueduct. The days were getting shorter, and it was dark by the time they arrived at the copper beech.

They sat down at their place and gazed at the river. They could see the lights of houses on the far shore, the lights of cars on the long bridge, and the lights of a tugboat in the channel. They could hear the sound of a train passing below them.

They had spent the day across the river, hiking the trail, looking for another unspoiled lake. They hadn't found one, but they had enjoyed being in the mountains, being free. By now she had realized that finding another unspoiled lake wasn't important. What was important was having the time to be together. So she wasn't happy about the fact that football practice was starting on Monday. Yet she knew he had to play, not only because of his father but also because of all the people, including her father and her brother, who expected him to play.

"I wish the summer was longer," she said.

"I wish it lasted forever," he said.

"You mean you don't want to go back to school?"

"I wouldn't mind going back to school. I wouldn't even mind playing football. I mean, if I could still see you."

"You can still see me."

"But not as much."

Of course he was right. When school started she would no longer be allowed to see him on weekday evenings, and because of football practice he would no longer be able to see her in the afternoons. And when it got colder they would no longer be able to make love here, at least without freezing their asses.

Taking advantage of the still warm weather, she kissed him invitingly.

For two weeks before school started, the football team had practice from ten to twelve in the morning, when they exercised and worked on fundamentals, and from two to four in the afternoon, when they ran plays and scrimmaged.

Kerry would get there around ten and sit in the stands and watch them, along with a few other spectators, mainly younger brothers and older people. She and an old man in a Giants cap never missed a session, and they developed a relationship based on their mutual interest in the team. The old man reminded her of her grandfather.

In the morning session they worked on the same things over and over. Brian, who was the quarterback, worked on taking the ball from the center, making hand-offs, and throwing passes. If she had been watching anyone else, she would have been bored.

At the end of the morning session Brian would take a quick shower and then meet her. They would go to her house and eat a sandwich and lie down on her bed and rest. They didn't make love, they just lay there and enjoyed being together, side by side.

In the afternoon session the team practiced a series of plays: through the line, around the end, a short pass over the center, and a long pass. And this was more interesting.

From what she saw, it looked like Brian was playing well.

"That was perfect," the old man said after Brian completed a long pass. "He has a good arm."

"Last spring he broke it," Kerry said.

"He did? Really? Well, it's all right now."

It evidently was, and knowing how he had worried about it, she was relieved.

On the Friday before school started they had a scrimmage with Gorton High School. It was like a game, and a number of people came to watch it, including her friends.

Gorton was in Yonkers, in another league, and they had bigger and better players. Within a few minutes they scored a touchdown.

"Oh, no," Amanda said. "This is going to be awful."

"I don't know why we play them," Susan said. "They always clobber us."

"The coach is a sadist," Lisa said.

"Come on, Brian," Kerry yelled.

Their team received the kick-off but only ran it back to the twenty. Brian tried a play through the line, which got nowhere, and then he tried a play around the end, which also got nowhere. So on third and ten, with no alternative, he tried a pass over the center. And Kevin, who was wide open, caught the ball and made a first down.

"That's the way," Amanda said, perking up.

"Come on, guys. You can do it," Susan yelled.

Brian ran a series of passes: another to Kevin, then one to Jason after faking to Kevin, and then a really long one to Kevin, who raced across the goal line.

Kerry and her friends cheered wildly. She looked around for Brian's father, hoping this would make him relent, but she didn't see him.

Gorton came back and moved the ball into their territory, but failed to score. And taking over, Brian ran another series of passes, using Kevin and Jason as receivers and finally hitting Kevin in the end zone.

They beat Gorton 35 to 14, and Lisa, who kept track of such things, informed them that Brian had completed all his passes, not missing a single one.

With Mark and Jerry the four girls waited in the parking lot for Brian and Kevin, who came out together.

"You were sensational," Amanda told them.

"It was Kevin who won the game for us," Brian said. "The way he was catching, I could have thrown him anything."

"But everything you threw was right to me," Kevin said.

"You know what got me started?" Brian said. "I heard Kerry cheering for me."

"Then keep cheering for him," Amanda said.

"We want you to keep hearing her," Susan said.

"Then you better put a gag on Lisa," Jerry said. "When she yells, you can't hear anyone else."

"My voice isn't that loud," Lisa said.

"It's pretty loud."

"Come on," Kevin said, opening the door of his car. "Let's go somewhere."

They all piled into the car and headed off.

Kerry was sitting on Brian's lap, with his arms around her. Since everything was going so well, she didn't mind that school started on Monday.

On Saturday morning, while she was cleaning the kitchen after breakfast, her mother called to her from upstairs: "Kerry, I want to see you."

She could tell from the tone of her mother's voice that something was wrong, so she went upstairs with trepidation.

"I'm in your room," her mother said.

She went into her room and found her mother standing near the bed. The top sheet had been stripped off, but the bottom sheet was still there.

"What are these?" her mother asked, pointing at the sheet.

"They look like stains," she said, cornered.

"Do you know where they came from?"

"I must have drooled there."

"You didn't drool in the middle of the sheet."

"Then I don't know where they came from."

"You do know. You were having sex."

"We weren't having sex, we were making love."

"On a sheet it looks the same," her mother said disgustedly.

"It's not the same. I love Brian, and he loves me. I'm going to marry him," she added, "and have his children."

"You're not going to marry anyone at the age of fifteen."

"I'm almost sixteen."

"The age of consent is seventeen. I could charge this boy with sexual misconduct."

"It was my idea."

"It was your idea to have sex?"

"No. It was my idea to make love."

Her mother sighed. "I warned you not to get too involved with him."

"I know you did. But I did nothing wrong."

"And what would Father Joseph say?"

"He'd say it was a mortal sin."

"Have you confessed it?"

"No. I haven't."

"You said it was your idea," her mother said after a silence. "So you decided to have sex with Brian. Can you tell me why?"

"I wanted to prove I love him."

"Do you think you did?"

"Yes. I did. And I made him happy."

"You can't make him happy."

"I can," she insisted.

"You can't, honey. You can give him temporary relief from his problems, but you can't solve them. Brian needs professional help."

"He doesn't. He needs me."

"You remember that boy I told you about? I thought I could help him, just as you think you can help Brian. But I couldn't help him."

"You could have if you'd really loved him."

"I did really love him. I loved him with all my heart and soul, but it wasn't enough."

She couldn't imagine her mother really loving anyone except her father, especially not a boy who got into drugs.

"I want you to stop seeing Brian."

"Well, what if I don't?"

"If you don't, then I'll bring charges against him."

"You wouldn't do that. It would hurt me."

"I will if I have to. And it wouldn't hurt you as much as he could."

"But I can't help seeing him at school."

"You know what I mean. I want you to stop seeing him alone."

"You mean forever?" she asked miserably.

"I'll tell you what," her mother said, relenting. "If you stop seeing him for three months, and if he sees a therapist, then we'll review the situation. But in the meantime you have to promise not to have sex with him."

"What if I don't?"

"I'll bring charges against him."

"Okay. I promise not to have sex with him." Of course that left the way open for her to make love with him since in her mind it wasn't the same.

Brian was coming to pick her up that evening, so her mother allowed her to see him in order to tell him what had happened.

They were still at the dinner table when the doorbell rang. She jumped up to get it, but Bobby was several steps ahead of her, and he was talking with Brian about the Mets by the time she could greet him.

With Bobby hanging onto his arm, he came into the dining room and politely said hello to her parents. Her father was as friendly as ever since her mother evidently hadn't yet told him what she had discovered, and even her mother acted the same with him. In fact, her mother acted as if she had a greater interest in him.

As soon as they were on the aqueduct she stopped and said: "My mother found out we're making love."

"She did? How?"

"There were stains on the sheet of my bed."

"Oh, shit. I'm sorry."

"She wants me to stop seeing you."

"What are you going to do?"

"I'm going to pretend to stop seeing you."

"I don't want you to get into trouble."

"Don't worry. I won't get caught."

"Okay," he said. "Then maybe it won't be so bad."

"She also made me promise not to have sex with you."

"What?" He looked distressed.

"But I didn't promise not to make love with you," she said. "It's not the same."

"It's not," he agreed readily.

"She said that if I stop seeing you for three months, and if you see a therapist, then she'll review the situation."

"She wants me to see a therapist?"

"She thinks you have problems."

"Well, I do have problems," he admitted. "But I don't need a therapist. I need you."

"My mother doesn't think I can help you."

"What do you think?"

"I think I can."

"You *have* helped me," he assured her, "and I've helped you. We've helped each other."

"I know we have."

"But if your mother wants me to see a therapist, I'll do it. I'll do anything it takes for her to let you see me."

"I will too."

"What about tonight?"

"We can meet at the party. That doesn't count because I won't be seeing you alone."

They kissed each other tenderly, and then they parted.

As she watched him go she knew she had hurt him, and she felt bad. Of course she believed it wasn't her fault, but blaming her mother relieved her feeling only a little, and she resolved to make up for what she had done to him.

ELEVEN

THE FIRST DAY of school was Tuesday, the day after Labor Day, and while they were standing in front of their lockers she told her friends what had happened.

"You're lucky," Amanda said.

"You are," Susan said. "If my mother found out that I'm making love with Mark, she'd put me in a convent."

"My mother would lock me up," Lisa said.

"Well, I'm going to keep seeing him," Kerry said. "But I need you to cover for me."

"We will. Don't worry," Amanda said.

"We know that if we were in your position, you'd do it for us," Susan said.

On her way to class she met Brian in the hall.

"I'm going to see Ms. Davis," he said after taking her aside.

"That's good," she said encouragingly.

"I'll meet you before I go to football practice, and I'll tell you what she said."

"Okay. I'll see you then."

She sat through English, and then through history, and then through lunch, thinking about him. She wondered what Ms. Davis would say.

When her study period was finally over she hurried down the hall and out the side door.

He was waiting for her.

"What did she say?"

"She said I need a family therapist."

"What's that?"

"It's a therapist who treats the whole family."

"Your parents would see him?"

"We'd all see him."

"Well, that makes sense."

"It does," he agreed. "But I can't imagine my father seeing a therapist."

"I can't either."

"Ms. Davis is going to talk with him."

"She is? That's good."

His father wouldn't do it, but Ms. Davis offered to meet with Brian once a week, so Kerry could tell her mother that he was seeing a therapist.

On Friday she and her friends went to the football game. They were playing Elmsford, which didn't have as good a team as usual, so they expected to win.

Sitting in the stands, they watched and cheered as Brian led their team in a series of plays to the Elmsford two-yard line. When he failed to score on the next play, sending Jason through the middle, Kerry heard a voice bellow: "No! No!"

She spotted Brian's father at the edge of the field, standing near the ball marker. If she hadn't known it was his father, she would have thought he was the coach.

"That's just what they were expecting!" his father yelled.

Brian glanced over at his father, and then at the coach, who motioned him to go ahead and call another play.

"Is that his father?" Amanda asked.

"Yeah," Kerry said, wishing he hadn't come to the game.

"He has a loud mouth."

"He should keep it shut," Lisa said. "He's not going to help by yelling at Brian."

She didn't think so either. She held her breath as their team lined up and Brian crouched behind the center. He got the ball, and it looked like he was sending Jason through the middle again.

"No! Not again!" his father roared.

Brian spun around, keeping the ball and deftly handing it to Tony, who by now was running at full speed around the end. His fake through the middle had drawn the defense, which couldn't recover in time to stop Tony from racing into the end zone.

Kerry and her friends jumped to their feet, cheering wildly.

"That'll show you," Amanda yelled at his father.

"You old fart," Lisa said.

But his father didn't keep his mouth shut. He stomped up and down the field with the ball marker, yelling at Brian on almost every play. And though they were leading by three touchdowns at half-time, he didn't let up.

Elmsford ran the kickoff back for a touchdown, and the next time they got the ball they scored again.

For a while both teams held each other, and then late in the final quarter Brian got their team moving. He was sending Jason through the middle, running Tony around the end, and making short passes to Kevin, taking no chances, slowly but surely driving into Elmsford territory, and eating up time.

With only a few minutes left to play, Brian dropped back to pass. This time instead of stopping short, Kevin went out long, and it looked like Brian was going to try for a touchdown. But then he turned and found Jason, who had suddenly appeared where he had been hitting Kevin. Since the Elmsford defender had followed Kevin, Jason was wide open.

He was about to pass to Jason when his father yelled: "No! You have a man open in the end zone! Pass it to him!"

Brian hesitated and looked at Kevin. Since he was being rushed, he had to get the pass off quickly. He looked back at Jason, who by now was covered, so he finally hurled the ball toward Kevin. Since he had been rushed and also rattled by his father, he didn't throw his best pass, and Kevin had to run for it, straining to catch it.

An Elmsford defender, a step ahead of him, stole it from him and started running in the opposite direction. It looked as if he would go all the way until Brian, cutting across the field, knocked him out of bounds. But now Elmsford had the ball.

"If his father had kept his mouth shut," Amanda said, "that wouldn't have happened."

"It wouldn't have," Susan agreed.

"I wonder whose side his father's on," Lisa murmured.

Kerry could imagine how Brian felt, and she hated his father for rattling him.

All fired up, Elmsford scored in three plays. So instead of winning the game as they should have, they had to settle for a tie.

She waited for Brian in the parking lot, along with her friends and Mark and Jerry. And when she saw him come out with Kevin, slouching toward them, she wanted to go and comfort him. But she held back, knowing he wouldn't want her to do that in front of people.

"Don't feel bad," Amanda told them. "You played a good game."

"I should have caught that pass," Kevin said.

"It was a bad pass," Brian said.

"No, it wasn't."

"Yeah, it was. It was my fault. I should have thrown it to Jason like we planned."

"You would have thrown it to Jason if your father hadn't yelled at you," Amanda said.

Brian looked at her, surprised. "You heard him?"

"We all heard him."

"They probably heard him in Dobbs Ferry," Lisa said.

"He rattled you," Mark said.

"Well, he didn't help," Brian admitted. "But it was still my fault. I made the decision to throw to Kevin."

"It wasn't your fault," Amanda said.

"It was your father's fault," Susan said.

"So how do we stop him from coming to games?" Lisa asked.

"We could ask the police to lock him up," Jerry said.

"For what?" Mark asked.

"For disturbing the peace."

They talked further about the problem, but that was as close as they got to a solution.

"Come on," Kevin said. "Let's go somewhere."

"We're going for a walk," Kerry said. She knew that Brian didn't feel like joining them.

As they watched the car drive off she put her arm around him and said: "It wasn't your fault."

"I feel like it was."

"I know. But it wasn't."

"Well, next time I have to ignore him."

"Pretend your father isn't there. Pretend I'm the only one watching you."

"I'll try that," he said hopefully.

"We should have won," Bobby said while they waited for their pizzas. They were at Sam's, which had been his choice since they had eaten Chinese last Friday. "Brian should have thrown to Jason instead of Kevin."

"Well, he was distracted," Kerry said.

"What happened?" her father asked.

"Brian was going to pass to Jason, who was wide open, but then his father yelled at him and told him to pass to Kevin."

"I thought that was Kevin's father," Bobby said.

"No, it was Brian's father."

"He should let the kids play," her father said. "He should stay out of it."

"I wish someone would tell him that."

"Do you want me to?"

"You should stay out of it," her mother said.

"The coach should tell Brian's father to keep his mouth shut," Bobby said.

"He should," Kerry agreed. "He has a right to make him leave, doesn't he?"

"Legally, he does," her mother said. "They're on school property."

"Then the coach should tell Brian's father that if he doesn't shut up, he has to leave."

"And if he doesn't leave," Bobby said, "the coach should beat the shit out of him."

"That's not a good way of settling disputes," her mother said.

"With some people, it's the only way," Kerry said, surprising herself.

"The coach should decide how to handle it," her father said. "It's his job to protect his players, even from their fathers."

On Saturday she told her parents she was going to a party at Lisa's house, and she did go there, but she met Brian there, and they left to go on the aqueduct. They walked to their place near the copper beech, where at least for a while she made him forget about the football game.

On Monday she went to football practice. She took her usual place in the stands, and presently she was joined by the old man in the Giants cap.

"That was too bad what happened on Friday," he said as they watched the boys trudge out from the locker room. "He set up that pass perfectly. He drew the defense out of the center with his right end, and then he slipped his halfback into the hole. He would have made a first down or even a touchdown. But then that fool yelled at him."

She was gratified to have her opinion confirmed by someone who knew football.

"The next time he should keep his mouth shut."

"He should," she agreed.

When the boys were all there the coach blew his whistle, and they gathered around him.

"You played a good game," he told them. "You have nothing to feel bad about. They got a break, and they took advantage of it. The lesson is, don't give the other team a break. Now, let's win the next one."

The next one was against Irvington, and with Brian calling a mixture of ground plays and passes, they scored the first time they had the ball.

Kerry had hoped that his father wouldn't be there, but he was there, stomping along the edge of the field with the ball marker, yelling at Brian as if he was doing everything wrong. But when

Brian passed to Kevin for a touchdown, his father's angry voice was drowned out by cheers.

They held Irvington, got the ball, and were driving for another touchdown when Brian, after hitting Kevin on two short passes, sent him out long. She not only recognized the play, but now that the old man in the Giants cap had explained it to her, she also understood it. She saw how the defense was drawn out of the center by Kevin, and how Jason slipped into the center, wide open. She held her breath as Brian acted like he was going to throw to Kevin, and then quickly turned to Jason.

"No! Throw it long!" his father yelled.

He passed to Jason, right to him, but for some reason Jason bobbled it.

"You should have thrown it long!"

"Oh, shut up," Amanda said.

"Yeah, let him alone," Susan said.

"You old fart," Lisa said.

It was now third down with one yard to go, and Brian sent Jason into the line. But he was stopped short of a first down, so they had to punt.

They held Irvington again, but only after giving up a lot of territory, and when they got the ball they were inside their own twenty.

Brian moved the ball to midfield, staying on the ground.

"You should pass it!" his father yelled.

He called another play on the ground, which got nowhere, and with ten yards to go, he had to pass. He hit Kevin on a short pass over the center, and then he sent Kevin out long. He cocked his arm as if he was going to throw to Kevin, who was wide open.

"Throw it short!" his father yelled.

He hurled the ball. With a slight wobble it traced an arc over the field and landed in the end zone, out of Kevin's reach.

"You should have thrown it short!"

On the next play Brian fumbled the snap from the center, and Irvington recovered.

A few minutes later Irvington scored.

"Come on, Brian," she cheered as they received the kickoff. She remembered how he had said after the scrimmage with Gorton that hearing her voice had gotten him started.

And it seemed to work. He led them back, sending Jason through the line and Tony around the end and making short passes to Kevin. He marched them down to the Irvington twenty. Then, for two plays, the defense held them.

On third down he dropped back for a pass.

"Now, don't blow it!" his father yelled.

"Come on, Brian," she cheered.

"Don't throw it over him!"

"Come on, come on."

"No, not to him!"

She watched in shock as the pass, which he had intended for Kevin, was intercepted.

The boy who caught it didn't get far, but he didn't have to. He had stopped them, and now Irvington had the ball. And after an eighty-yard drive they scored.

That was the turning point. From then on Brian couldn't get them moving again. He couldn't get anywhere on the ground, and he couldn't pass. When he threw another interception, which led to an Irvington touchdown, the coach took him out and put in the second-string quarterback, a sophomore named Larry. And Brian sat on the bench for the rest of the game.

When it was over the coach went and confronted his father. She couldn't hear what they were saying, but she supposed that the coach was asking him to keep his mouth shut. His father scowled, and then made a gesture with the back of his hand.

"I wish the coach would hit him," Amanda said.

"I do too," Susan said. "Right in the mouth."

"If he did, then Brian's father would sue him," Lisa said.

Kerry said nothing. She imagined how Brian felt as he hobbled to the locker room.

"Well, I don't care if he is your son," the coach shouted at his father. "He's my quarterback. So lay off him."

"You can't tell me what to do," his father roared back. "I pay your salary. And if you were doing your job, I wouldn't have to yell at him."

"I'm doing my job."

"Then why did you lose?"

"You were riding my quarterback."

"You lost the game because you don't know what the fuck you're doing."

Restraining himself, the coach turned away from him.

"You ought to be fired," he yelled at the coach.

The coach ignored him.

"What a shit," Amanda said.

"If he was my father, I'd run away," Susan said.

"I'd kill him," Lisa said.

Kerry said nothing.

By the time Brian came out of the school there was no one else around. She had told her friends not to wait, so they had gone off in Kevin's car. And she was standing outside the door, ready to comfort him.

His head was bowed as if he couldn't face the world after what he had done. And when he looked up she saw the anguish in his eyes.

She went to him and put her hand on his shoulder. "Don't feel bad. It wasn't your fault."

"It was."

"It wasn't. If your father hadn't yelled at you, we would have won."

"But we didn't win."

"It doesn't matter. What matters is, we love each other."

He smiled. "Yeah. That's what matters."

They started walking down the hill with their arms around each other's waist.

"Did your father always yell at you like that?"

"He always yelled at me, but not like that.'

"So why is he doing it now?"

"I don't know. I guess because I'm not playing well."

"But you *are* playing well until he yells at you."

"I'm not playing well."

"You are. I mean, look how well you played against Gorton. And he wasn't there."

"That was a scrimmage. It wasn't a game."

"Well, if he's not the problem, what is?"

"I don't know. It could be my arm."

"Does your arm bother you?"

"No. I mean, it doesn't hurt. But maybe it didn't heal right. And maybe that's why I'm not passing as well as before."

"You didn't miss one pass against Gorton."

"I guess I didn't. Then I don't know what the problem is."

"Are you sure it's not me?"

He shook his head. "It's not you. If I didn't hear you cheering for me, I couldn't do anything."

She was reassured.

That evening she had go to out for dinner with her family, and she poked at the crispy shrimp with her chopsticks while her father and her brother talked about the game. She stayed out of the conversation, and when they got home she went up to her room and closed the door.

Lying on her bed, she worried about Brian. She still believed she could help him, but now she realized what she was up against. She had to overcome his father's influence, and since the war was being waged on a football field, she knew she was at a disadvantage. While his father yelled at him with authority, she could only cheer for him.

She believed that in the long run she would win the war against his father since Brian wanted to be a psychologist, not an athlete, but she was concerned about what might happen in the short run if his father kept riding him.

Her mother opened the door and came in, advancing to the side of her bed and looking at her. "Are you all right?"

"Yeah," she said faintly.

"You were quiet at dinner."

"I didn't feel like talking."

"It sounds like Brian's father is giving him a hard time."

"He is. He keeps yelling at him."

"And you feel bad because you can't help him."

"I *can* help him. I just don't know if I can help him win a football game."

"How could you?"

"By cheering for him."

"If that worked, then every team would win."

"But we should win, and if his father didn't yell at him, we would win."

"Why does his father yell at him?"

"I don't know. I guess he wants Brian to play well."

"But yelling at him doesn't help him."

"No. It hurts him."

"So maybe his father really doesn't want him to play well."

"Why would his father not want him to play well?"

"Maybe his father's jealous of him."

"Why would he be jealous?"

"Brian has his whole life ahead of him, and maybe his father regrets what he did with his own life."

"His father had a contract with the Red Sox, but he gave up playing when Brian was born."

"Well, that might explain it."

"He blames Brian, and he blames Brian's mother. You should hear how they talk."

"Then I was right about his needing to see a therapist. Has he done anything about that?"

"Yeah. He met with Ms. Davis. She said his family should see a therapist, but his father wouldn't do it. So Brian's seeing her once a week."

"I hope that helps," her mother said as if she had doubts that it would.

On Monday, when they met in the hall during recess, he said:

"Ms. Davis thinks I should sit out the next game."

"Do you think that would help?"

"It wouldn't hurt. I mean, it wouldn't hurt the team."

"If you don't play, would your father leave?"

"I don't know. I guess he would."

"Then why don't you try it?"

"I'll ask the coach and see what he thinks."

The coach thought it was a good idea. In fact, they agreed that Brian wouldn't even dress for the game but would sit in the stands with Kerry and her friends.

When the teams lined up for the kickoff his father looked around for him, not seeing him on the field or on the bench. He finally spotted him and marched over and stopped in front of them, red with anger.

"Why aren't you playing?" his father demanded.

"I don't feel like it," Brian said.

"Are you sick?"

"No. I just don't feel like playing."

"You mean you're chicken."

Brian tensed.

She put her hand on his shoulder, afraid he might jump up and attack his father.

But he restrained himself.

"You're afraid to go out and fight like a man," his father roared. "So you're hiding with the girls."

"Lay off him," Kerry said in a voice that surprised her.

His father glared at her. "What did you say?"

"She said to lay off him," Amanda said.

"Are you deaf?" Susan said.

"Down in front!" the old man in the Giants cap shouted. "We're here to watch a football game. And you make a better door than a window."

Other people joined him, shouting: "Down in front!"

"It's your fault," his father growled, looking at her bitterly. And then he stomped off.

Though she knew he was only being spiteful, his remark

affected her. It made her wonder if she was really helping Brian.

"Hey, we got rid of him," Amanda said.

"He's going to his car," Lisa said.

Kerry said nothing. With her hand on Brian's shoulder she could feel his tension, and she was still afraid he would go after his father.

A few minutes later the coach came over and said: "He's gone. You can suit up now."

"Okay. I'm ready," Brian said through clenched teeth.

As he got up she clasped his hand, saying: "I'm with you all the way."

"Yeah, show the old bastard," Amanda said.

"You have what it takes," the old man in the Giants cap said.

When he came out dressed for the game they rose to their feet and applauded him.

"Come on, Brian," she cheered with all her heart.

After sending Jason through the line he threw a perfect pass to Kevin, then one to Jason, then another to Kevin, and finally another to Kevin in the end zone.

That was the first of six touchdowns, against a team that wasn't bad. As she watched him she knew he was driven by anger. At one point after being rushed he ran with the ball and hit a tackler so hard that the boy had to be carried from the field on a stretcher. Imagining what he might have done to his father, she was glad he was on the football field.

When he came out with Kevin after the game they were all waiting in the parking lot, and they all congratulated him.

Taking him aside, she said: "That proves it wasn't your fault. The problem was your father."

"I guess it was," he said reflectively.

"Come on," Kevin said. "Let's go somewhere."

"Let's go to Brian's house," Jerry said, "and tell his father how well he played."

"That's not a good idea," Amanda said.

"We want his father to think he quit playing," Lisa said.

"So his father won't come to the games?" Jerry asked.

"That's right," Lisa said, patting his shoulder.

"Hey, that's clever. Whose idea was it?"

"Ms. Davis and the coach worked it out," Brian said.

"Are they going with each other?"

"They're both married," Amanda said.

"Ms. Davis suggested that I sit out the game," Brian said, "and the coach used that to get rid of my father."

"The coach is smart," Kevin said.

"So you're going to let your father think you quit playing?" Mark asked.

"I don't see how else I can get him off my back."

Kerry didn't either. But she knew that his father would give him a hard time for quitting. She also knew that his father would blame her.

An hour later they were on the path below his house when she saw his father coming down the steps toward them.

"You better go," Brian told her.

"I'm not going to leave you," she said, holding her ground.

"But he's going to be nasty. I can tell."

"I don't care. I'm not afraid of him."

"There you are," his father said, advancing toward them. "Where have you been? Fucking your brains out in the bushes?"

"Don't talk that way," Brian told him.

"You don't tell me what to do. I tell *you* what to do."

"You can't make me do anything."

"I can make you stop seeing this little cunt."

"Tell her you're sorry," Brian said, stepping between them.

"I'm not sorry. She's a little cunt."

"I'm going to beat the shit out of you."

"Stop it!" his mother screamed from the top of the stairs, where she was standing in a white nightgown. "I can't stand it!"

Brian froze with his hand raised against his father.

"You're chicken," his father taunted him.

"I'm going to kill you."

"Stop it! Stop it!" His mother started wailing as if it was the end of the world.

Brian looked from his father to his mother, torn between them, and then he lowered his hand and said: "Come on, Kerry."

Before going she said to his father: "He's not chicken. *You* are. You make him want to kill you, but you know he won't because of her."

"You're full of shit."

She ignored this remark and went with Brian.

They walked for a while in silence, and then he said: "I shouldn't have let him get away with calling you that."

"It's just a name. It didn't hurt me."

"I still shouldn't have let him get away with it."

"Don't worry. I understand why you didn't hit him."

"When she wails like that, I can't stand it."

"I know. But don't think about it. Thank about how you're going to help other people."

"That's in the future. What about now?"

"Now," she said, putting her arm around him and drawing him close, "think about how we're going to spend the next hour at the copper beech."

"Okay," he said, brightening.

THE NEXT GAME was against Tarrytown, and as they drove there she hoped his father wouldn't show up. But a few minutes after the kickoff she saw him take his usual place at the edge of the field with the ball marker.

"Oh, shit," Amanda said.

"He must have heard how they tricked him," Lisa said.

Knowing she was in a war with Brian's father, Kerry got up and walked to the ball marker. She stood next to his father and shouted: "Come on, Brian!"

His father scowled at her, but in front of all those people he couldn't do anything to her.

Her friends came and joined her, and they went up and down the field with Brian's father, making such a clamor that even they couldn't hear him. And Brian gave them plenty to cheer about. He passed to Kevin for a touchdown, he ran for another, and then he passed to Jason for another.

By the third quarter they were comfortably ahead, but Brian didn't let up. He played as if he wanted to silence his father once and for all.

He was carrying the ball, coming around the end toward them, when a Tarrytown player cut him off and drove him out of bounds. It happened right where they were standing, and it looked like he was going to run into his father.

But his father got out of the way, and Brian, who had lost his balance, crashed into the stands behind them.

"Oh, no," she cried, rushing toward him.

When he struggled to his knees he was holding his right arm.

"Did you break it?" she asked.

"I don't know," he said, obviously in pain.

"Let me see it," his father said.

"No. Don't come near me."

"Just let me see it."

"Lay off him," she told his father.

His father turned on her, glowering. "Are you telling me what to do?"

"Yes. I am. I'm telling you to lay off him."

"I am too," the coach said, behind her. "Lay off him. And let us get him to a hospital."

"I'll have you fired."

"Go ahead. How does it feel?" the coach asked Brian.

"It hurts," he said, stretching his arm out. "But it doesn't feel broken."

"Well, I don't want to take any chances. Who has a car?"

"I have a car," his father said.

"Who else has a car?"

"If you think you can stop me from driving my own son to the hospital—"

"I don't think I can stop you. I know I can."

"You have no right to interfere."

"I sure do. I've seen how you treat him, and I don't trust you to drive him to the hospital."

"I'll sue you," his father roared. "I'll sue the school."

"Go ahead. Now, who else has a car?"

"I have a car," Amanda said.

"Then you take him. And don't mind this big bully. If he gives you a hard time, I'll kick his ass around the field."

Kerry helped Brian get to his feet.

"You played a great game," the coach said, patting him on the butt. "You won it for us. So you don't have to hurry back."

"Come on," Kerry said, putting her arm around him.

They headed for the parking lot while his father raged at the coach.

They drove to St. John's and went to the emergency room.

Though there were only a few people ahead of him, Brian had to wait for a long time.

Kerry sat next to him, supported by her friends.

"Brian Donahue?" a woman called out.

She gave his hand an encouraging squeeze and watched him go through a door.

"Do you think he broke it?" Susan asked.

"I know he hurt it," Amanda said. "He landed pretty hard."

"He almost ran into his loud-mouth father," Lisa said.

"I wish he had," Susan said. "He probably wouldn't have hurt himself. He only would have hurt his father."

"We should have stopped his father from getting out of the way," Amanda said.

Kerry said nothing. She wondered what they were doing to him now. She prayed that his arm all right, though she was fully prepared to hear that he had broken it again. If he had, then he couldn't play football, and that would get his father off his back. So it wasn't the worst thing that could happen to him.

Brian finally appeared, wearing a sling.

She jumped up and met him.

"I didn't break it," he told her.

"What did you do to it?"

"I tore some ligaments."

"What does that mean?"

"It means I can't play football for a while."

She was glad he hadn't broken his arm, but she was just as glad he couldn't play football for a while. And he didn't look unhappy about it.

When she got home her family was ready to go out for dinner, and she apologized for being late.

"Where were you?" her mother asked.

"My friends and I took Brian to the hospital."

"What happened to him?"

"He was driven out of bounds," Bobby said, "and he crashed into the stands."

"Good lord," her mother said. "How is he?"

"He's all right. But he tore some ligaments in his arm."

"You mean he can't play?" Bobby asked.

"He won't be able to play for a while," his father said. "It takes as long for ligaments to heal as a broken bone."

"Come on," her mother said impatiently. "You can talk about it in the car."

"That doesn't count as seeing him," she told her mother as they drove away. "I wasn't alone with him. I was with my friends."

"It doesn't count," her mother agreed. "Did he keep playing after he got hurt?"

"No. But if his father had gotten his way, he might have kept playing."

"What do you mean?"

"His father wanted to see the damage, but Brian wouldn't let him. And the coach wouldn't let him. We told his father to lay off him."

"You told his father that?"

"I did. When he broke his arm playing basketball," she explained, "his father acted like it was nothing. That's why he kept playing."

"Then he wasn't trying to be a hero?"

"He's not that way."

"Then maybe I was wrong about his motives." Her mother didn't have to say: "But he still has problems."

"His father threatened to sue the coach," Bobby said.

"He did? What for?" his father asked.

"For letting the girls drive him to the hospital."

"Well, I don't think his father will sue anyone. People with loud mouths hardly ever do what they threaten to do."

Kerry wasn't worried about what his father might do to the coach. She was worried about what he might do to Brian—and about what Brian might do to him.

On Saturday night she went to Lisa's, and Brian just happened to come there.

"What? No cast?" Jerry said.

"You don't have a cast for torn ligaments," Lisa said.

"But I wanted to sign it."

"You can sign his arm," Kevin said.

"I wouldn't let him sign my arm," Amanda said.

"Will you be out for the rest of the season?" Mark asked.

"Yeah. I will," Brian said. "The doctor said it takes about six weeks for ligaments to heal."

"Well, let me tell you," Kevin said, patting his back. "You're the best quarterback we ever had. And yesterday you really showed them."

"I just threw the ball. You're the one who caught it."

Kerry said nothing. She had no words to express her admiration for Brian. But later, while they were dancing, she put her arms around him and pressed her face against his shoulder, letting him know how proud of him she was.

With his arm in a sling between them, it was like the first time they had danced, and she was almost glad that he had hurt his arm again.

On Monday he went to football practice, and she went with him. They sat in the stands, along with the old man in the Giants cap, and they watched the team run plays with Larry as quarterback.

"He's good," Brian said after Larry had completed a pass to Kevin.

"He's not as good as you," the old man said.

"Well, give him a chance. He's only a sophomore."

Kerry agreed with the old man, but she said nothing since she didn't want Brian to feel any pressure to play. She wanted him to sit back and relax.

After a while he said: "Come on. Let's go for a walk."

They left the field and headed for the aqueduct.

It was October, and the leaves were turning. A few trees were already yellow as if the fall had touched them first. And others were fading.

As they walked along the aqueduct they could feel the change in the wind.

They stopped at her house so she could drop off her books. They stayed for a while, eating cookies, and then somehow they started kissing.

She could tell how much he wanted her, and she finally said: "Let's go upstairs."

"What about your brother?"

"He won't be home until after five."

"Are you sure?"

"I'm sure. Come on," she said, taking his hand.

They went up to her room, and to avoid leaving evidence she covered the bottom sheet with an old towel, which she could hide from her mother and throw away when she no longer had any use for it.

For the next two weeks they went to her house directly after school and made love in her bed. He had to leave before Bobby got home, but they still had two hours together, and during that time he forgot about his problems. Instead, he talked about his hopes and dreams, and listening to him, she believed more firmly than ever that all he needed was her love.

Then one day, while lying in her bed, they both fell asleep.

The next thing she knew, her brother was calling: "Kerry? Kerry?"

She sat up quickly.

"Are you all right?" The door was closed, and Bobby was on the other side of it.

"Yeah. I'm all right. I was taking a nap."

"Can I come in?"

"No. I don't have any clothes on," she said truthfully.

"Okay," he said, retreating.

Brian looked at her for guidance.

"We better get dressed," she whispered.

They slipped out of bed and found their clothes, hers on a chair and his on the floor.

"I'll distract him while you get away."

"Where did he go?"

"He went to his room."

"Okay," Brian said. "I'm ready."

She kissed him goodbye, and then she went out into the hall. The door to Bobby's room was open, and she went in, closing it behind her.

"Why did you close the door?" he asked. He was lying on his bed, reading a sports magazine.

"Oh, I didn't mean to. I did it out of habit."

"Yeah, you always close the door to your room."

"I like to have privacy."

"You said you were taking a nap."

"I was. I'm having my period. It always makes me tired."

He made a face and returned to his magazine as if he didn't want to know about such things. "Do you always take a nap without clothes on?"

"Yeah. You should try it some time."

"What did Brian do today?"

"How should I know? I'm not allowed to see him."

"But you must hear about what he's doing."

"I don't hear anything."

"Well, I hope he'll be able to play before the season ends."

"We don't need Brian. We won the last two games without him."

"They were easy teams. We have to play Dobbs Ferry a week from Friday. And without Brian we won't have a chance."

"Sports aren't everything," she said. She glanced out the window and spotted Brian on the path, heading home. And she was relieved.

During the week of the Dobbs Ferry game he met her in the hall at school and said: "I'm going to play the last two games."

"I thought it took at least six weeks for ligaments to heal."

"It's been three weeks, and my arm feels fine."

"Is your father putting pressure on you?"

"He wants me to play. And he says there's nothing wrong with my arm."

"He doesn't know. He sent you back into a basketball game when your arm was broken."

"This time I didn't break it."

"I know. But you tore the ligaments. And my father says it takes as long for ligaments to heal as a broken bone."

"My father says I didn't tear the ligaments."

"The doctor said you did."

"He says the doctor's full of shit."

"That's what he said about your mother's doctor," she said, remembering the remark his father had made coming upstairs.

"He doesn't have any use for doctors."

"So what does he say you did to your arm?"

"He says I only twisted it. He says I'm faking."

"Why would you be faking?"

"So I don't have to play."

"Don't you see? He's just saying that to make you play."

"But he could be right."

"Then ask the coach."

"Okay. I will."

The coach advised him to see the doctor at Lenox Hill who had treated him for the broken arm. At first the woman who answered the phone said the doctor couldn't see him until early November, but after he had explained how urgent it was she agreed to fit him into the schedule the next day.

Kerry got her homeroom teacher to let her out of the study period early so that she could go to the city with Brian, and they took the two-fifty-five train.

When he came back into the waiting room after seeing the doctor Brian said: "Well, that settles it."

"What did he say?"

"He said I shouldn't play sports for another three weeks."

"So your father was wrong."

He nodded. "Yeah. I asked the doctor to call him and tell him. But I don't know if that will get him off my back. He'll probably say the doctor's full of shit."

That was what his father did say. But with her and the coach and the doctor on his side, he was able to resist his father's pressure, and he sat out the Dobbs Ferry game, which they lost by two touchdowns.

It was Saturday, and they were hanging out at Amanda's house. Amanda was painting her toenails, Susan was dancing, Lisa was reading a magazine, and Kerry was gazing out at the river.

"I'm glad the football season has ended," Amanda said.

"Did Kevin feel bad about losing?" Susan asked.

"Yeah, for a while. But he got over it."

"When you're at the game it seems important, but later it doesn't."

"It's not important," Lisa said.

"It's really not," Amanda said. "If it was, they wouldn't get over a loss so easily."

"Did Brian feel bad about not playing?" Susan asked.

"Yeah," she said, turning from the window. "But he knew he couldn't, so he accepted it."

"I think it was good that he hurt his arm," Amanda said.

"It relieved the pressure," Lisa said.

"But it didn't solve the problem," Kerry said.

"You mean his father?"

"His mother's just as bad in her own way."

"Then he should get away from them."

"He will when he goes to college. But in the meantime he has to live with them."

"Well, at least the football season has ended."

"But basketball season has begun," Susan said.

"I've had enough of sports," Amanda said.

"If the voters had turned down the school budget," Lisa said, "they might have eliminated sports."

"I wish they had," Susan said.

Kerry did too. She wasn't looking forward to the basketball season since there would be pressure on Brian again.

Later that afternoon, as she was going upstairs to take a shower, her father called to her from the family room. "Kerry?"

She stopped.

"I want to talk with you."

From the tone of his voice she knew what had happened. Somehow they had caught her.

Feeling sick, she went to face the consequences.

His father was with Bobby, watching a football game on television, and when she got there he asked Bobby to go out and rake leaves.

"Can I just watch the end of the game?"

"No. You can't."

Without another word of protest Bobby left the room.

Her father closed the door behind him, turned off the game, and faced her.

She waited in dread for him to speak.

"Are you seeing Brian?"

"I see him every day at school."

"You know what I mean. Are you having sex with him?"

"We're not having sex. We're making love."

"Whatever you call it," her father said, "you promised your mother not to do it."

"I promised not to have sex," she argued. "I never promised not to make love."

"Let's not split hairs. You know what your mother wanted from you."

"But we're not just having sex. We love each other."

"You broke a promise," her father said.

Kerry had nothing further to say in her defense. She knew that in her father's eyes breaking a promise was one of the worst things you could do. And afraid that she had lost his respect forever, she started to cry.

"If you couldn't keep your promise," her father said less harshly, "you should have told us, instead of coming here after school behind our backs."

"I'm sorry," she said, bawling.

"We still love you. Whatever you do, we'll love you. But we

want to trust you, and we want you to trust us. We only want the best for you."

"I know," she said, wiping her eyes.

"So don't lie to us, and don't make promises you can't keep. And don't try to be a lawyer. We already have one in the family."

She smiled, feeling that the worse was over.

"Now, what are you going to do about Brian?"

"I have to see him. He needs me."

"You don't have to have sex with him."

"I'm not having sex with him. I'm showing him I love him."

"There are other ways to show a person you love him."

"I guess there are. But if I stop, then he'll think I don't love him anymore."

"You never should have started. You're not old enough to handle it."

"But I did start. And I *am* old enough. Why would I be able to make love if I wasn't old enough to handle it?"

"We're able to do a lot of things we can't handle."

"Well, I don't see how I could make him understand."

"Would you like me to talk with him?"

"If you did talk with him, what would you tell him?"

"I'd tell him you're not old enough to handle making love with him. I'd tell him that if loves you, he'll wait until you're old enough."

"He does love me."

"If he does, he can show it by abstaining. He can prove he loves you by respecting the fact that you're only fifteen."

"I'm almost sixteen."

"But even then you'll be under age."

"Mom threatened to charge him with sexual misconduct."

"Don't worry. We wouldn't do that. Your mother was trying to get your attention. But there's a reason for the law."

"What's the reason?"

"To protect young people," her father said, "to prevent them from getting hurt."

"Brian would never hurt me. He loves me."

"He could still hurt you."

"I don't see how."

"I do. And your mother does."

"Okay," she said after considering her options. "I'll talk with Brian. I'll tell him what you just said about waiting until I'm old enough."

"I think he'll understand."

"Can I ask you a question?"

"Sure. What?"

"How did you find out that I was seeing him?"

"I ran into his father at the supermarket. His father said he saw you with Brian on the path below their house. He said he asked you to stop seeing Brian."

"Not exactly," she said, remembering the name his father had called her. "But he did see us together on the path."

"So I asked Bobby if he had seen you with Brian. For a while he lied to protect you, but I finally got the truth out of him. When I told your mother, she searched your room, and she found a towel hidden in your closet." Her father had the good grace to stop there.

Her parents allowed her to meet Brian on the aqueduct so she could talk with him. Since she wanted privacy, she arranged to meet him at their place near the copper beech, and she found him there sitting and gazing at the river.

By now the leaves were falling, and the foothills on the other side were turning brown. The water was gray, reflecting the sunless sky above. Though the walk there had warmed her up, she was glad she had worn her fleece-lined jacket.

She sat down next to him and put her arm around him, saying: "May parents found out what we've been doing."

"I was afraid they would."

"My father thinks we should stop making love."

"Did he ask you to promise to stop?"

"No. He asked me to talk with you," she said. "He thinks I can convince you that we should wait until I'm old enough to handle it."

"He thinks you're not old enough to handle making love?"

"That's what he thinks."

"What do you think?"

"I don't know. I wish I was older."

"You mean you think your father could be right?"

"He could be. He said there are other ways I can show you I love you."

"I guess there are," he said thoughtfully.

"According to our religion," she said, "we're not supposed to make love until we're married."

"I know we're not. I hope you don't feel bad about it."

"I know I've committed a sin, but it didn't feel like a sin, so I really don't feel bad about it."

"That's good." He was silent for a while, and then he said: "Well, I can live without making love with you. But I can't live without you."

"You don't have to live without me. My parents said I could see you as long as we're not making love."

"Then we'll abstain," he said, finding her hand and holding it.

"I love you," she said, laying her head on his shoulder.

"If you didn't love me, I'd jump off the bridge."

"No, you wouldn't."

"Yeah, I would."

"Then I'd jump after you."

"You would?"

"I would." She hadn't taken him seriously, but she believed that knowing she would jump after him would stop him from even thinking about it.

THIRTEEN

ON MONDAY AFTERNOON he stopped at her house after basketball practice for cookies and milk. They were in the kitchen when Bobby came in. Bobby immediately produced a ball and asked Brian to help him with his shots. And Brian went outside with him.

Kerry sat on the steps and watched them, remembering the first time Brian had helped her brother. She had liked him for it then, and she loved him for it now.

When her father came home he changed and joined them as he always had. He was very aggressive, and at one point when he had the ball he drove through Brian, knocking him aside and making a layup.

Bobby, pretending to blow a whistle, called a foul.

"What do you mean?" his father objected.

"That was charging."

"No, it wasn't."

"It wasn't," Brian said graciously.

"I guess it was," her father admitted. "I'm sorry."

"Forget it. I was in your way."

After that her father stopped being so aggressive. In fact, he started being very polite. But he didn't act the same as he had before they found the towel.

Kerry and her friends were in the stands, waiting for the first basketball game to begin. Brian's father was there in the front row, ready to yell at him.

"Come on, Brian," she cheered as the referee was about to toss the ball up.

Brian got it and passed it to Mark, who scored on a jump shot.

She kept cheering, and he kept playing well. Of course his father was yelling at him, but it didn't affect him. It was as if he had tuned out his father and could hear only Kerry and her friends, who cheered along with her.

At the end of the third quarter, with a comfortable lead, the coach took him out of the game.

"It's to save his arm," Amanda said.

"The coach knows what he's doing," Susan said.

But his father didn't think so. After yelling in vain at the coach for a while, he left in disgust.

"Good riddance," Amanda said.

"He acts like he doesn't want Brian to play well," Lisa said.

"That's what my mother says," Kerry said.

"Why wouldn't he want his own son to play well?" Susan asked.

"Because he's jealous," Kerry said. "He's an old fart, and Brian's young."

"Well, it doesn't affect Brian anymore," Amanda said, patting her on the shoulder.

She felt like she had won a battle against his father.

They waited for him and Mark in the parking lot, and then went off in Kevin's car.

While the others trooped into McDonald's she and Brian stayed in the car, and looking into his eyes, she said: "You did it."

"You helped me."

She smiled, feeling vindicated.

"My father doesn't affect me anymore because I'm not playing for him. I'm playing for you. So I don't hear him, I only hear you."

"And my friends," she said, giving them credit.

"That's what Ms. Davis said I should do. She said that if I'm going to play, I should do it for a positive reason. And you're the reason."

Happily, she hugged him. She felt like she had won the war.

Brian's parents didn't celebrate Thanksgiving because they felt they had nothing to be thankful for, so she asked her parents if he could join them for dinner that day. Her mother said no, it was a family holiday, but she said he could go to Sam's with them on Friday. Without saying so, her mother made it clear that this was a reward for being good.

They took a walk that afternoon, but they didn't stay long at their place near the copper beech because it was barely above freezing now. They stopped at his house around five so that he could change his clothes and look presentable to go out for dinner with her family.

He was upstairs, and she was waiting for him in the living room, when his father came home.

"What are you doing here?" his father asked her rudely.

"I'm waiting for Brian. He's changing his clothes."

His father scanned the sofa with disgust. "It looks like you were fucking him here."

"I wasn't," she said. "I wasn't doing anything."

"I know what you were doing with him, you little cunt."

At that point she saw Brian coming down the stairs.

"Take that back," he told his father, approaching him.

"What if I don't?" his father taunted him.

"I'll kill you."

"Sure. You won't even hit me."

Brian faced him, quivering with rage. "Now, take it back."

"Come on," she said, reaching for his hand.

"Go with her," his father said. "And fuck your brains out. But I can tell you what'll happen. She'll get pregnant, and then you'll have to marry her."

"Is that what happened to you?" she asked.

"Yeah. His mother refused to have an abortion."

"I thought she was an atheist."

"She wasn't then."

"Well, that's not going to happen to us. We're abstaining."

His father laughed. "Sure you are. If I wasn't here, you'd be lying naked on the sofa with your legs spread and your pussy wide open."

"Tell her you're sorry, you didn't mean that," Brian said, letting go of her hand.

"Make me," his father challenged him.

Brian took a swing at his father and hit him in the jaw, sending him toward the fireplace.

"You little shit," his father said, recovering and grabbing the poker.

"Stop it!" his mother screamed from the landing of the stairs.

"Make me take it back," his father snarled, brandishing the poker.

Brian hesitated, unable to ignore his mother.

"What's wrong? Are you chicken?"

"He's not chicken," Kerry said.

"Stay out of it," his father said. "You've already done enough damage, you little cunt."

"I'll kill you," Brian said, advancing toward his father.

His father swung the poker, which Brian blocked with the arm he had injured twice before. And Kerry winced, imagining what the blow had done to it.

Brian punched his father in the stomach and knocked the wind out of him.

"Stop it!" his mother screamed.

With his father reeling, Brian was about to hit him again when his mother started wailing. And that stopped him.

Before his father could recover he said: "Come on. Let's go."

They left the house and went down the steps to the aqueduct, where they paused to catch their breath. He was holding his arm as he had after he tore the ligaments.

"I think you should go to the emergency room," she told him.

"Maybe I should, but not now. I'm going away."

"Where are you going?"

"Across the river."

"Then where?"

"As far away as possible."

"But what about school? What about college?"

"I can go to college later. Right now," he said, "I have to get away from them. I can't live with them anymore."

"What about money?"

"I can get a job."

She knew he needed her, and she believed what he had said, that he couldn't live without her, so without a moment's hesitation she said: "Wherever you go, I'm going with you."

"Are you sure you want to go with me?"

"Yes. I'm sure."

"What about your parents?"

"They'll understand."

"Then I'll go to Mark's and get my car while you go home and get what you need. I'll meet you at Mark's in a half hour."

"Okay. I love you."

"I love you too."

While she walked to her house she decided to wait until she was packed and ready to go before she told her parents what she was doing.

She opened the door and tiptoed in. She paused and listened. She heard her parents in the kitchen, talking. It was almost time for them to leave and go to Sam's, and they were probably wondering where she was.

She crept upstairs, mentally listing the things she needed.

In her room she gathered them and laid them on her bed: underwear, socks, another top, and of course her toothbrush. She would have liked to take her pink sweater, but for some reason she felt that she had to get everything into one bag.

When she was ready she went downstairs. She left the bag in the front hall and went into the kitchen, where she found her parents sitting at the table, having a drink.

"What's wrong?" her father asked.

"Everything," she said, trying to hold back her tears. "Brian just had a scene with his parents, and he can't live with them anymore."

"What's he going to do?"

"He's going to run away, and I'm going with him."

"Do you really think that's a good idea?" her mother asked her calmly.

"No, I don't. But I don't know what else to do. I can't let him go without me."

Her father looked at her mother, who nodded at him in resignation.

"You say he can't live with his parents," her father said. "Could he live with us?"

She couldn't believe what he was suggesting. "Live with us?"

"Like a member of the family."

"He could have my office as a bedroom," her mother said. "I've decided to stop bringing work home."

"His father would probably sue us," her father said, "but your mother could handle it."

Kerry thought about it. If Brian lived with them he would be like an older brother, as to some extent he already was. And that would be good for him.

"Do you want to try it?" her father asked her.

"Yeah. I do."

"Where is he now?"

"He's at Mark's house, where he keeps his car. He's waiting for me to meet him there."

"I'll take you there. Come on."

When they arrived there she didn't see Brian's car. They had agreed to meet there in a half hour, and checking her watch, she saw that she had been on time.

"He's not here," she told her father.

"Well, maybe he changed his mind about running away."

"I don't think he did. I can't imagine him going back to his house."

"Then maybe he went to our house to pick you up."

"Maybe." But she wondered. Had he gone without her after deciding that it wouldn't be good for her to leave home?

"Let's go and see," her father said.

They turned around and went back to their house, but Brian wasn't there either.

"He went without me," she concluded.

"Do you want to go after him?" her father asked.

"Well, I don't know if we can catch him, but I want to try."

"He can't be too far ahead of us." With squealing tires her father put the car into motion and headed up Broadway. He ran the light at the Grand Union and rounded the corner at a speed that pulled her against the door.

When they passed Mercy College the speed limit went up to forty, and her father went faster.

Approaching the bridge, they saw the flashing lights of police cars, and she wondered if his father had asked them to set up a barricade.

"If he's ahead of this," her father said, referring to the backed-up traffic, "we might not catch him."

They slowed, then stopped, and then inched ahead.

"It looks like there's been an accident," her father said.

She had a sudden, horrible thought. But she immediately dismissed it.

There were two police cars: one on the bridge, and the other on the causeway.

When they finally reached the one on the causeway her father rolled down his window and asked the policeman who was standing there: "Can you tell me happened?"

"There's been an accident,"

"On the bridge?"

"Yeah. Someone jumped off it."

"Oh, my God," she cried, guessing what had happened.

"Do you know who it was?" her father asked the policeman.

"I can't tell you. Now, please move on."

"I think it was Brian," she told her father.

"My daughter thinks it was someone she knows."

The policeman peered through the open window. "Do you know a Brian Donahue?"

Kerry said nothing.

"Yes. We know him," her father grimly. "Can you tell us what he did?"

"According to a witness," the policeman said, "he stopped his car on the bridge and got out. He took off his jacket and climbed over the rail and jumped."

"God damn him," her father said.

"That's all I know. If you can tell us more, we'd appreciate it. Just pull over."

Her father did. He shut off the engine, unhooked his seatbelt, and put his arm around her, saying: "It's not your fault. The boy had problems, serious problems."

"Yeah. I know."

"You tried to help him. You loved him, you encouraged him. You did everything humanly possible."

"I know," she said, pretending to believe it.

"Come on. Let's get out."

She got out of the car, and with her father's arm around her she walked toward the policeman. He was reaching into his car for something, and when he pulled it out she saw that it was Brian's jacket. The policeman asked: "Do you recognize this?"

"Yeah. That's his."

At that moment his father arrived, escorted by another policeman. "Where's my son?"

"He's in the river. He jumped off the bridge."

"What the fuck are you talking about?"

"He jumped off the bridge," the policeman repeated.

His father looked wildly down at the river. "No, he didn't. He wouldn't do a thing like that."

"He evidently did. He, or someone, got out of his car and took off this jacket—"

"Let me see it," his father said, grabbing it. He held it up and examined it, and then he flung it back at the policeman. "Why didn't you stop him?"

"We weren't here. We're down there now, looking for him. But I have to tell you, he couldn't last long in that cold water."

"Why didn't you get here sooner?"

"We got here only a few minutes after we received the call."

In a rage his father turned on her. "Where were *you*?"

"With me," her father said.

"Why weren't you with him?"

"She stopped at our house to get her things. They were going to run away."

"Was that your idea?"

"It was his idea."

"You're the reason he killed himself," his father bellowed, pointing a finger at her.

"Take it easy," the policeman warned him.

"*It's all your fault.*"

"God damn you," her father said, smacking him hard across the face.

With a bloody mouth his father reeled back.

"*You're* the reason," her father said. "You drove him to it. You made him want to go away. And that's what he did. He went as far as he could go."

"You don't know what happened," his father snarled.

"Whatever happened, it wasn't her fault. And if you say *one more fucking word*, I'm going to knock you off the bridge."

"Easy, easy," the policeman said, stepping between them.

His father glared at her, wiping his mouth.

"Come on," her father said, putting his arm around her and guiding her away.

As she opened the door she paused and stared down at the river. It was still and black, like the end of all hope, the end of all love, and the end of all life.

She was sprawled on her bed with her face in the pillow when her mother came in.

Her mother sat down on the bed and laid a hand on her back. "I know how you feel. You feel that if only you'd said or done the right thing, you could have saved him."

"If I'd really loved him, I could have."

"You couldn't have. And you did really love him."

"Then why didn't he believe it?"

"I don't know. I guess after what his parents did to him, he couldn't believe it. He couldn't believe that anyone could love him."

"But I should have proved it."

"You did prove it. You were willing to run away with him."

"Then why didn't he wait for me?"

"I think," her mother said after a moment, "he was driven by something stronger than his love for you."

"What do you mean?"

"His hate for his parents. I think his jumping off the bridge proves that he hated his parents more than he loved you."

She remembered telling him that if he jumped off the bridge she would jump after him. Obviously, he hadn't believed her. If he had, he wouldn't have done it. "Well, my love for him should have stopped him."

"His love for *you* should have stopped him."

"It would have," she said, "if he'd believed I loved him."

"If he didn't believe that," her mother said, "it was his fault, not yours. You did everything humanly possible."

That was exactly what her father had said. But she didn't believe it. She hadn't done enough to prove she loved him. And now it was too late. The only thing she could do now was prove it to herself.

FOURTEEN

"KERRY," HER MOTHER called from the doorway. "It's after ten. It's time to get up."

She had been trying to go back to sleep, putting off the time when she would have to face what had happened, and still hoping that when she woke up again she would find that it had only been a nightmare.

"Amanda called. She's coming to see you."

"I don't feel like seeing anyone."

"I know you don't. But it'll help to talk with her."

She didn't see how. She didn't see how anything would help.

"I'll be in my office if you need me."

She raised herself. She swung her legs over the bedside and found her slippers. She tottered into the bathroom and sank down onto the toilet and closed her eyes, overwhelmed by sorrow. She wished she could just go down the drain.

Back in her room, she paused at her window and gazed out at the river. The blue water was flecked with whitecaps, churning from the opposition between the current and the rising tide. The Palisades were dusted with snow.

She had always loved the river and had felt privileged to have a view of it, but now she hated it, as she hated and feared the thought of death.

She put on some clothes, not caring what she wore or how she looked. She brushed her hair perfunctorily. And then she went down to the kitchen.

She poured some apple juice and got a doughnut. Sitting at the table, she took a bite of the doughnut and a sip of juice, but she immediately felt sick. It was as if her body, going along with her mind, had decided to reject anything that would keep her alive.

She was roused by the doorbell, and only out of consideration for her mother she went to answer it. When she opened the door she saw her friends.

They had tears in their eyes.

Amanda stepped forward and hugged her, crying: "I'm so sorry."

Susan and Lisa stood there, crying.

"How did you know?" Kerry asked them.

"I heard it on the radio," Amanda said.

"What did they say?"

"They said a boy jumped off the bridge. And then they gave his name. I couldn't believe it."

"I still can't believe it," Susan said.

"Did they say anything about finding him?"

"They said they hadn't."

For a moment she had a wild hope that he had survived the fall from the bridge and the cold water, and that he had reached the shore and proceeded on foot, letting his parents think he was dead in order to punish them. But then she realized that if he had survived he would have let her know, and the hope faded.

She led her friends into the kitchen, and they sat down at the table. She offered them doughnuts, cookies, and milk, but they declined.

"What happened?" Amanda finally asked.

She told them everything, including what Brian's father had said on the bridge and what her father had done to him.

"It's about time someone smacked him," Amanda said.

"Good for your father," Susan said.

They lapsed into a silence.

Then Lisa said: "I think he did it to hurt his father."

"I do too," Amanda said. "He hated his father."

"But he should have thought of you," Susan said.

"He should have known it would hurt you," Lisa said.

"He knew how much you loved him," Amanda said.

"He didn't," Kerry said. "He didn't believe I loved him."

"How could he not believe it?" Susan asked.

"You gave him everything," Lisa said.

"If he'd thought of you for one moment," Amanda said, "he wouldn't have done it."

Kerry said nothing.

At church on Sunday she followed her brother into the pew and knelt down and closed her eyes, with her forehead against her clasped hands. She prayed for only one thing—that Brian had survived. She was even willing to accept the punishment of never seeing him again if only he was still alive.

Before beginning the mass Father Joseph said: "If you haven't heard the sad news, a boy from our village took his own life on Friday evening. We don't know what he was feeling, but he must have felt that life was unbearable. I know that at times you might feel that life is unbearable, but when you do, remember that God gave you life, and that God will never abandon you. God is your father, your perfect father. God is your mother, your perfect mother. And you are His children, you are the reason He created the world."

Reinforcing this message, her father put his arm around her.

"In the name of the Father, and of the Son—" the priest said, making the sign of the cross.

Automatically, she made the sign of the cross.

When she came back from receiving communion she knelt and again prayed for that one thing. She promised to dedicate her life to God if He would only answer her prayer.

The next day, while she was she was staring at a book during study period, she was called to Ms. Davis's office. She didn't want to talk with Ms. Davis, but she had no choice.

"Please sit down," Ms Davis said gently.

She sat down, folding her arms and bowing her head.

"I'm sorry about Brian."

Kerry said nothing.

"I was trying to help him," Ms. Davis said. "And I know you were too. So we must have a similar feeling."

"What do you mean?"

"We feel like we failed him."

"I did fail him."

"You didn't fail him. You feel like you did, but you didn't. There was no way you could have saved him."

"If I'd really loved him I could have saved him."

"Where did you get that idea?"

"I don't know."

"Well, it's a delusion," Ms. Davis said. "No matter how much you love someone, you can't save him."

"Then what's the use of loving him?"

"You can give him the opportunity to love you. And if he does, he can save himself."

"You mean if he'd loved me he wouldn't have done it?"

"No. He wouldn't have."

"So if I'd made him love me—"

"You can't make people love you. They either love you or they don't love you. And if they've grown up without ever seeing an example of love, they probably won't."

"But they could."

"Oh, yes, after years of living. But even then," Ms. Davis said, "it's not likely, and at Brian's age it wasn't going to happen no matter what you did."

"I still feel like I failed him."

"I know you do. But it had nothing to do with you. He did it because he hated his parents, and he wanted to hurt them in the worst way."

"How do you know?"

"From listening to him. I mean, he talked about killing his father. And he said he wished his mother would die. But then they wouldn't have suffered anymore. So it would hurt them more for him to kill himself."

"Did you think he might kill himself?"

"I thought he might, and I tried to prevent it."

"So that's why you feel like you failed him?"

"Yes. But I'll get over it, and you will too. Instead of blaming ourselves or his parents, we should blame Brian for what he did. It was an act of hatred."

"He didn't know what he was doing."

"He knew damn well what he was doing," Ms. Davis said. "He was doing the ultimate number on his parents. And he didn't care what it did to you."

"That's what my friends say."

"You're friends are right."

She had been in her room and was coming downstairs to help her father make dinner when she heard her parents in the kitchen, talking.

"How's she doing?" her mother asked.

"She's feeling a lot of pain," her father said. "I hate that boy for hurting her."

"I hate myself for letting it happen."

"You didn't let it happen. You tried to stop her from getting too involved with him."

"Well, maybe by trying to stop her I caused her to go farther than she would have if I'd stayed out of it."

"You didn't cause her to do anything," her father said.

"I just wish she hadn't had sex with that boy."

"But if she hadn't, she might blame herself now for holding back on him."

"She might," her mother said. "At least this way she can feel she did everything she could have for him."

"She's not there yet," her father said. "She still feels it was her fault. And his father didn't help by telling her it was her fault, the fucking bastard."

The next day, while she was in the stationary store with her friends, she saw on the front page of the regional newspaper: "BODY FOUND IN RIVER."

She didn't have to read the story to know it was Brian's body they had found.

Her friends hadn't seen it, and she didn't tell them.

When she parted with them she went to the aqueduct and started walking. She remembered the times he had met her on the path, and she closed her eyes, praying that when she opened them she would see him there.

Approaching his house, she saw his mother at the window, and on an impulse she went up the steps and knocked on the back door.

A few minutes later the door opened, and his mother appeared in the usual white nightgown, not looking happy to see her. "What do you want?"

"I want to know if you're going to have a funeral for Brian."

"Why should we have a funeral for him?"

"So he can rest in peace."

"He's resting in peace," his mother said. "At least that's what I believe. You probably believe he's gone to hell for killing himself."

She felt like telling his mother that Brian had killed himself to escape from the hell of living with his family. But it wouldn't have helped his mother, and it wouldn't have helped her. She only said: "I don't believe that."

"Well, if he *is* in hell, you sent him there."

"I didn't," she protested. "You did."

Blinded by tears, she left his mother and stumbled down the steps. She continued walking, already sorry for saying something that would hurt his mother.

She went through Dobbs Ferry and across the campus of Mercy College. She went as far as the copper beech. With her shoulders hunched and her hands stuck in the pockets of her coat, she stood and looked at the ancient tree, which had given them shelter. Its branches, now picked clean by the wind, were like bleached bones.

She went to the place where they had made love for the first time. There was no evidence that they had been there, no mark, no imprint. The ground was hard, impervious.

Whatever her mother or her friends or Ms. Davis had said,

she still felt it was her fault. If she had really loved him, he would have believed it. And if he had believed it, he wouldn't have killed himself.

His father was right. It *was* her fault. And there was only one way she could redeem herself.

She gazed at the bridge. She couldn't imagine standing on the edge and looking down and having the courage to jump. She would do it from the pier in Henley, where she could throw herself into the water.

She shivered at the thought.

But it wasn't as bad as the thought of having to live with herself.

On her way back through the village she stopped in front of Our Lady of the River. She imagined going into the church and confronting God, but she knew it wouldn't be open now, so she stopped in front of the Blessed Mother, crossed herself, and said: "Holy Mary, Mother of God, pray for us sinners now and at the hour of our death."

There was no response from the statue.

She continued walking on Warburton and headed down Spring Street. She passed the health food store, still feeling bad about quitting her job after Jeanne had been so nice to her, and she went down to the train station.

She crossed the bridge that went over the tracks and walked between the abandoned buildings of the Anaconda Wire & Cable Company. She knew the way since she had gone there a number of times, always with a group of friends.

When she reached the pier she stopped and looked around. There was no one in sight, no one to stop her.

She moved to the edge and stared into the murky water. She would finally prove she loved him. She would keep her promise. She would follow him where he had gone. If he was in hell now because he had killed himself, she would join him there.

She was about to jump when she heard the voice of Our Lady of the River, saying: "Kerry, my child. Killing yourself is not an act of love. Living your life is. So go home to your family."

As she stepped back from the edge she imagined how her parents would have felt if she had done it. She imagined how her friends would have felt. And she finally realized that if Brian had loved her, he wouldn't have done it.

She also realized that Ms. Davis was right. No matter how much you loved someone, you couldn't save him. If he loved you, he could save himself. But if he didn't, it wasn't your fault since you couldn't make people love you.

She turned from the river and headed home.

Her father and Bobby were shooting baskets.

As she went through the gate her father stopped and hailed her, holding the ball.

"I'm home," she said, beginning to cry.

He dropped the ball and met her as she rushed to him. And he held her tight as she sobbed her heart out and confessed what she had almost done.

"Thank God," he said, hugging her.

"I love you," she said. "That's what stopped me. That's what saved me."

"Is she all right?" her mother said, coming out the back door. It wasn't even six, and her mother was home, already changed out of her work clothes.

"Yeah, she's all right," her father said, letting her go.

She went to her mother and faced her, saying: "I'm sorry, mom."

"What for?" her mother asked.

"For thinking you didn't really love that boy. Now I know you did. And now I know that what happened wasn't your fault."

Her mother smiled, and in her human face was a look of unconditional love.